HEAR YE! HEAR YE!
THE GRAND DUKE OF
THORTONBURG ANNOUNCES
THE JOYFUL DISCOVERY
OF A DAUGHTER, VICTORIA,
AND GIVES HIS BLESSING
TO HER BETROTHAL TO
SIR LANCE GRAYSON

LET IT BE KNOWN that a "king's ransom" led to the Grand Duke's discovery of his daughter, **VICTORIA**, a courageous woman who stood her regal ground against her captors…and fell in love with Captain Lance Grayson…

LET IT BE KNOWN that **LANCE GRAYSON**, newly knighted "Sir," completed his royal mission with honor—and even took a bullet for his royal bride-to-be! (Note to Sir Lance: Next time…shining armor…)

LET IT BE KNOWN that the long-standing plague—ahem, feud—between the houses of Thorton and Montague is over. (And at last check, no more surprise heirs were on the royal radar screen. But one never knows….)

Dear Reader,

♪♫ "Happy Birthday to us...." ♪♫ Exactly twenty years ago this May, Silhouette Romance was born. Since then, we've grown as a company, and as a series that continues to offer the very best in contemporary category romance fiction. The icing on the cake is this month's amazing lineup:

International bestselling author Diana Palmer reprises her SOLDIERS OF FORTUNE miniseries with *Mercenary's Woman*. Sorely missed, Rita Rainville returns to Romance with the delightful story of a *Too Hard To Handle* rancher who turns out to be anything but.... Elizabeth August delivers the dramatic finale to ROYALLY WED. In *A Royal Mission*, rescuing kidnapped missing princess Victoria Rockford was easy for Lance Grayson. But falling in love wasn't part of the plan.

Marie Ferrarella charms us with a *Tall, Strong & Cool Under Fire* hero whose world turns topsy-turvy when an adorable moppet and her enticing mom venture into his fire station.... Julianna Morris's BRIDAL FEVER! rages on when *Hannah Gets a Husband*—her childhood friend who is a new dad. And in *Her Sister's Child*, a woman allies with her enemy. Don't miss this pulse-pounding romance by Lilian Darcy!

In June, we're featuring Dixie Browning and Phyllis Halldorson, and in coming months look for new miniseries from many of your favorite authors. It's an exciting year for Silhouette Books, and we invite you to join the celebration!

Happy reading!

Mary-Theresa Hussey

Mary-Theresa Hussey
Senior Editor

Please address questions and book requests to:
Silhouette Reader Service
U.S.: 3010 Walden Ave., P.O. Box 1325, Buffalo, NY 14269
Canadian: P.O. Box 609, Fort Erie, Ont. L2A 5X3

A ROYAL MISSION
Elizabeth August

Silhouette
ROMANCE™
Published by Silhouette Books
America's Publisher of Contemporary Romance

Special thanks and acknowledgment are given to
Elizabeth August for her contribution to the
Royally Wed series.

To romance writers everywhere
Happy Millennium!

 SILHOUETTE BOOKS

ISBN 0-373-19446-3

A ROYAL MISSION

Copyright © 2000 by Harlequin Books S.A.

Visit Silhouette at www.eHarlequin.com

Printed in U.S.A.

Books by Elizabeth August

ELIZABETH AUGUST

lives in the mountains of North Carolina with her husband, Doug, a chemist. They have three grown sons. Their oldest is pursuing a career in medicine, their middle son is a chemical engineer and their youngest is now in college.

Having survived a bout with cancer, Elizabeth has now joined the ranks of cancer survivors. Writing remains at the top of her list of loves just below her husband, sons and daughter-in-law. Elizabeth has also written under the pseudonym of Betsy Page for Harlequin.

THE THORTONS

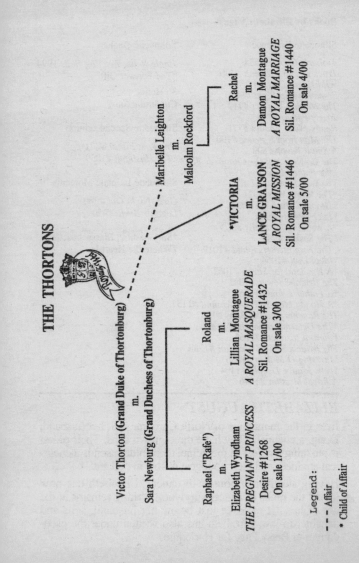

Victor Thorton (Grand Duke of Thortonburg)
m.
Sara Newburg (Grand Duchess of Thortonburg)

Maribelle Leighton
m.
Malcolm Rockford

Raphael ("Rafe")
m.
Elizabeth Wyndham
THE PREGNANT PRINCESS
Desire #1268
On sale 1/00

Roland
m.
Lillian Montague
A ROYAL MASQUERADE
Sil. Romance #1432
On sale 3/00

*VICTORIA
m.
LANCE GRAYSON
A ROYAL MISSION
Sil. Romance #1446
On sale 5/00

Rachel
m.
Damon Montague
A ROYAL MARRIAGE
Sil. Romance #1440
On sale 4/00

Legend:
- - - Affair
* Child of Affair

Chapter One

Using only the full moon to light his way, Lance Grayson moved stealthily through the woods. His destination was the one-room cabin ahead. Its porch roof sagged in one corner and its windows were boarded up. Weeds, underbrush and small trees were reclaiming the clearing in which it sat. Pausing, he used night-vision binoculars to survey the scene in front of him. The place looked totally abandoned. Silently, he cursed. Time was running short for finding Victoria Rockford, and it looked as if this lead was a dud. Even worse, it was his only lead.

He adjusted the binoculars to survey the woods surrounding the cabin. Four of his best men were forming a perimeter circle. In a lowered voice, he spoke into the headset he was wearing, calling each man by name.

Each responded with, "In position, sir."

So we all get some practice doing night reconnaissance, he told himself, trying to look on the bright side. It didn't help. The photo he had of Victoria Rockford haunted him. She looked so alive, so vital, her face a strikingly beautiful version of the Thorton features. That she could die because he did not find her soon enough, tore at his very soul. It bothered him that this assignment seemed more personal, more urgent. He was normally much cooler, much more detached.

Aloud he said, "Hold your positions. Looks like a wild-goose chase, but I'm going to see it through as if our quarry is here."

Making his way to a side window of the cabin, he looked through one of the spaces between the boards. With only slender rays of moonlight illuminating the interior, he could see very little. He was lifting the night-vision binoculars to his eyes when he heard it…a soft moan. Peering through the binoculars, he allowed triumph to flow through him. On a bed in a far corner lay a woman, handcuffed to the brass headrail, her feet bound with rope to the footrail.

"Looks like this might not have been a wild-goose chase after all," he told the others. "The princess appears to be alone. I'm going in."

Victoria Rockford fought the drugs she'd been given to sedate her and tried to focus her thoughts.

Her struggle proved futile. Her mind remained foggy and the temptation to give in to sleep grew stronger. Her movements slow and weak, she closed her hands around the brass poles of the headboard and gave a jerk on the rope that bound her feet to the brass footrail of the bed. She'd done this a hundred times before. Each time she'd hoped that the bed would finally give way, crumble to pieces and allow her to escape. It hadn't. She wanted to scream in frustration, but the gag in her mouth prevented that. Mentally, she cursed "The Whisperer," the name she'd dubbed her kidnapper, and vowed vengeance should she ever get free. *When* she got free, she corrected herself, refusing to consider the alternative.

Hearing a footfall on the porch, she froze. An adrenaline rush brought some clarity to her sluggish mind. Her captor came twice a day to feed her and to allow her to use the facilities. Blindfolded so that she could not tell if it was day or night, her sense of time had been severely affected. Still, she was certain it was too soon for him to be returning. Normally, by the time he came, the drugs had worn off enough that she had more coordination. Had the time come to find out why she'd been kidnapped? Fear threatened to overwhelm her. Her jaw clenched. She would not go down without a fight.

The door squeaked, signaling that it was being opened. She lay perfectly still, gathering her energy for one final battle. The footfalls approaching her were softer, more cautious than usual. Had her captor sent someone new? Maybe this person would not be so careful.

A beam of light shone on her face.

"Miss Rockford, I'm Captain Lance Grayson," a man said, switching the light off before working her blindfold loose. "I'm here to help you."

Victoria blinked several times before she was able to focus. Even then, with only the moonlight, she could make out very little about the man in the cabin. He was dressed all in black and wearing the sort of high-tech gear she'd seen on SWAT teams in cop movies. She wanted to believe he was here to rescue her, but she wasn't ready to trust anyone. Her being kidnapped didn't make any sense. What did the kidnapper have to gain? Her father, Malcolm, wouldn't pay a penny to see her safe. Of that she was certain. Until she knew what was going on, she would remain on her guard.

The man finished removing the gag, then tossed it aside. Next he produced a small kit of lock-picking tools and unfastened the handcuffs. While he worked, he checked in with his men. Assured the perimeter was secure and that no one was approaching, he ordered his jeep brought to the front of the cabin.

Victoria wondered if she were having a drug-induced dream, or maybe even an hallucination. It seemed as if she had been in the cabin forever. Maybe her mind had snapped.

Having freed her hands, the man took out a knife and cut the bonds holding her feet. "Can you sit up?" he asked, easing her into an upright position.

Her head swam and nausea threatened. This was no dream. A nightmare, maybe. But no dream. "I don't feel so good," she murmured, her hands fastening around his upper arm for support. The muscles beneath her palms were granite hard. Even in her drugged state a curl of feminine excitement wove through her. In the next instant, it was replaced by a rush of fear. If he should turn that strength against her, she would have little chance of surviving. As she cursed her continued weakness and inability to coordinate her movements properly, her head lolled forward and came to rest on the arm she was clutching.

"You're going to be fine," the man assured her. Then he scooped her up in his arms and carried her outside to the waiting vehicle.

His strength stunned her while the heat of his body flowed through her, combating the chill in the night air. No longer did she doubt his existence. Her imagination was good, but not that good.

Fighting a fresh wave of grogginess, she peered hard at his face when he settled her on the passenger side and fastened her seat belt. His features were angular and set in a grim expression with no hint of even the barest softness. He was what she would expect her kidnapper to look like, not her rescuer.

Fear rippled through her. Like the good-cop, bad-cop ploy she'd seen used on television police dramas, maybe her kidnappers were playing a game with her. Maybe, for some reason, they needed her cooperation now and thought this was the way to get it.

"I noticed her suitcases are inside. Get them and toss them in the back of my jeep," the man ordered a subordinate who had driven the jeep to the front of the cabin.

Victoria looked to see who her rescuer was talking to. His companion, too, was dressed all in black. In her dazed state he appeared a shadow image, the kind that drifted in and out of nightmares, scaring the dreamer. A shiver shook her.

She heard her proclaimed rescuer again talking to others through the headset he wore. Looking toward the woods, she saw no one else. Were there other shadowy helpers, or was that part of the game? she wondered. It was hard to think. Sitting back in her seat, she closed her eyes and tried to will her mind to clear and her body to regain its coordination. The endeavor proved too exhausting and darkness encompassed her.

Hoping that at least one of the kidnappers would show up to be captured, Lance issued orders for his men to remain and keep watch over the cabin. "And now to get you to a safe location," he said to Victoria, climbing into the driver's seat. Receiving no response, he looked to his companion. She was slumped forward.

Concern swept through him. He felt her pulse. It was beating slowly but regularly. He checked her breathing. It, too, was regular. "Miss Rockford." He spoke her name tersely.

Her eyelids appeared too heavy to open. "Water," she requested, her voice hoarse.

Lance grabbed a flask and held it to her lips.

Never opening her eyes, she drank her fill, then slumped against the seat.

Satisfied she was merely in a drugged sleep, Lance drove away from the cabin. Still, he could not stop himself from continually glancing at her. The worry that there could be more wrong with her than merely the effects of drugs taunted him. He frowned. Emotions dulled a person's instincts, made them unreliable. He didn't like that. He was a man used to being in total control; a man who had trained himself not to allow anything to distract him from his purpose.

The road was uneven and he hit a pothole, jarring the vehicle. Victoria surfaced with a groan. "My head," she moaned. In the next instant she was asleep again.

"That does it," he growled, unable to fight what felt very close to panic for her well-being. Pulling over to the side of the road, he again checked her pulse and breathing. Lifting her eyelid, he flashed a light in her eyes. The pupils were even and reactive.

From the emergency medical training courses he'd taken, he knew all signs pointed to simple drug-induced sedation. Still, this time, with this patient, he would be more thorough.

Victoria once again became semiconscious, her demeanor fearful. "What's going on?"

"I was just checking to see if you were all right."

Victoria clamped her mouth shut.

The thought that she had incredibly kissable lips flashed into Lance's mind. *Thoughts like that are totally unprofessional,* he admonished himself sternly and turned his attention back to the business at hand. "Were you hit on the head? Did you sustain any other blows?"

She seemed to concentrate. "I don't think so," she said at last.

Lance studied her face for bruising, then gently ran his fingers through her hair to feel for any lumps on her head. As the long dark tresses wove through his fingers, they produced a seductive effect that threatened to vanquish his mission from his mind. Quickly satisfying himself that she had no lumps or bruises, he broke the contact.

The gentle massage of his fingers had a soothing effect, and Victoria found herself wanting to purr. When he stopped, she felt deprived. *He could be making certain you're in good enough shape for whatever evil he still has in store for you,* she cautioned herself, angry that she'd allowed the delicious feel of his touch to weaken her guard. For all she knew, he could be The Whisperer. This last thought sent a chill through her.

He opened a water flask and held it to her lips. "Drink," he ordered.

This time prudence won out over thirst. "No."

"You need the water to wash the drugs out of your system," he coaxed.

Her thirst was growing stronger. She'd drunk before and the water had been drug-free, she reminded herself. Still, she refused to trust the man beside her. "You drink first."

He smiled, a pleased expression in his eyes, giving the impression that he approved of her behavior. Raising the flask to his lips, he took a swallow.

Deciding the water was safe, she allowed herself to drink. As they pulled back onto the road, her mind seemed to clear a bit and the hope that the drugs were wearing off flowed through her. Testing her body, she tried shifting in her seat. The attempt required a huge expenditure of energy and produced few results. *I just need a little nap,* she told herself, closing her eyes.

It was daybreak when Lance arrived at his cottage on the northwestern shore of the island nation of Thortonburg. No one knew he owned this place. It was a part of his life he'd kept entirely private. Lifting Victoria out of the jeep, he carried her inside and found himself thinking that she felt very good in his arms. Immediately, he scowled at himself.

That was not a thought he should be having about this woman.

"Bathroom," Victoria murmured against his shoulder.

Carrying her into the facility, Lance stood her on her feet.

She was wobbly and obviously nauseous, but she was determined to take care of her needs in private. "I can do this by myself," she said tersely.

Lance wasn't convinced, but he backed out into the hall. "I will leave the door open. If you think you may fall, yell."

He heard her sluggish movements, then the sound of splashing water.

"Are you finished?" Lance asked, worried she would fall and seriously injure herself.

"Yes," she replied.

Entering the bathroom, Lance found her holding on to the sink as if to keep from crumpling into a heap on the floor. He scooped her into his arms and strode to the bedroom where he gently laid her on the bed. He removed her shoes, then tossed a light cover over her. Finally he went outside to retrieve her suitcases from the jeep and brought them to the bedroom.

Standing beside the bed watching her sleep, he noted that her color was returning and that her breathing was deeper. With luck the drugs would soon be out of her system.

He showered quickly, then dressed in slacks and

a pullover shirt. After checking to see if his guest had awakened and noting that she hadn't, he made himself some breakfast. But instead of eating in the kitchen, he carried his food into the bedroom. There, he sat in a chair watching Victoria Rockford as he ate. Fury toward the men who had done this to her grew more and more intense. He vowed he would not rest until Malcolm Rockford and his accomplice were captured. And Lance and the Thortons were more than convinced Malcolm was the self-proclaimed "Justicier."

Again, the thought that he was taking this case much too personally taunted him. "It's my duty to find those men," he countered tersely under his breath, needing to speak the words aloud to assure himself they were the truthful reason behind his feelings. Victoria Rockford could never be anything other than someone he was duty-bound to protect.

Victoria turned onto her back and stretched. A smile played at her mouth. She'd been dreaming that she'd been rescued. A ruggedly handsome face, cold and unsmiling, filled her mind. Her smile vanished. *Rescued, or merely changed prisons?* She frowned. *Silly girl. It was just a dream.* She stretched again. Her breath locked in her lungs. She was able to move freely. Opening her eyes, she raised her hands upward and looked at them. Her bonds were gone.

More alert now, she realized she was lying on a much softer, much more clean-smelling bed. She opened and closed her eyes a couple more times to bring them into clearer focus. Sunlight streamed through an open window and the room smelled of sea breezes. Was she still dreaming?

Her gaze traveled around the room. The decor was masculine and a little stark, but she liked it. Turning her head as far to the right as she could, her whole body suddenly became rigid. Seated in a chair near the bed was the man she had been dreaming about. He was no longer dressed all in black or equipped with the high-tech equipment, but the face…the stern, cold-featured face…was the same. And he was armed. He wore a leather shoulder holster that housed a very dangerous-looking weapon. She thought she saw a momentary flash of relief in his eyes as he rose and approached the bed, but her guard remained strongly in place.

"Would you like some water?" he asked.

She recalled that he'd given her water before and it had been safe to drink. Attempting to ease herself into a sitting position, she was assailed by a wave of dizziness. She squeezed her eyes shut to fight the sensation.

"Are you all right?" the man asked with cool composure.

"Dizzy," was all she could manage to reply.

"That's a natural reaction after having been drugged." Seating himself on the side of the bed, he slipped his arm behind her shoulders and eased her up so that she could swallow. "Drink. The fluid will help."

Victoria obeyed. As the bout of dizziness subsided, she became acutely aware of the strength of the arm holding her. Although a great deal of the past days remained a blur, that part...the sturdiness of her rescuer...she remembered vividly. The thought that if he was on her side she would never have to be afraid again filled her mind.

He waited until she'd drunk as much as she wanted, then laying her down gently, he asked, "How do you feel now?"

"Like my body is a two-ton weight," she replied honestly, the struggle to shift herself continuing to require tremendous effort.

"That, too, is natural. I'll bring you some soup."

She noted that he spoke to her in an efficient, factual manner, politely but with no emotion. *Friend or foe?* She could not be sure. Whichever he was, he wasn't worried about her escaping, she noted. He left her free of bonds when he exited the room.

Long ago she'd vowed that she would not passively accept whatever fate life dealt her. Determined to regain her strength and coordination so that if she must fight for her freedom she would at least have a chance, she forced herself into a sitting position, her legs dangling off the side of the bed. The movement helped. Her body felt a little less leaden.

Still, her neck remained so weak, her head drooped downward until her chin rested on her chest. Drawing in a deep breath, she grimaced at the whiff of body odor. She needed a bath. Even more importantly, nature was again calling. Easing herself off the bed, she stood beside it. Her legs felt rubbery. When she tried to walk, she tottered and was forced to grab hold of one of the rear posters for support. "Rats!" she cursed in frustration. "And mice! And snakes!"

Lance was pouring the soup into a pan when he heard her. He raced back to the bedroom, fear for her jolting him as he entered. She was pale as a sheet and looked as if she was going to fall any second. "You're not strong enough to walk around on your own yet," he barked, reaching her in long strides.

"That part I figured out," she returned curtly.

"You need to lie back down." He tried to loosen her grasp on the bedpost so that he could get her back on the bed.

Victoria refused to budge. "What I need is to use the facilities."

"You have spunk. Most people in your condition, both men and women, would still be lying flat on the bed and yelling for help." He hesitated a moment, then added, "All right. Let go of the post and I'll take you there."

Acutely aware of his arm across her back and his hand holding her at the waist, she released her hold. His touch had a curiously invigorating effect as if she was gathering strength from him. When he placed his other hand in front of her, offering it for further support, she took hold and began to move forward, out of the room. For someone so strong, he was incredibly gentle. And she thought she'd seen real concern in his eyes when he'd come bursting into the room.

Straightening a little to maintain her balance, she glimpsed his gun and a chill of fear curled through her. *Don't be too quick to trust him,* her inner voice cautioned. *He could simply be under orders to see that you're not injured for the time being.*

"You said something about mice and snakes? Did you see any?"

Realizing he was worried that she was hallucinating, Victoria smiled dryly. "No. My parents never allowed my sister and I to use profanity, so when we would feel the need to curse we would name things we found disgusting."

They had reached the bathroom, and Victoria released her hold on him and took hold of the doorjamb. "I can take care of myself from here."

He regarded her doubtfully.

She glared up at him. "I insist."

Carefully, he freed her.

Using the wall for balance, Victoria entered the bathroom and closed the door, but instead of reveling in her privacy, she found herself missing her host's support. With her forehead pressed against the wall for stability, she unfastened her pants, pushed them and her panties down, then sat. The drugs were definitely wearing off. Her movements, although still sluggish, were more coordinated.

With her elbows on her knees, she rested her head in her hands. Memories of her incarceration in the cabin flooded over her. Being escorted by her current host had been a great deal different than being escorted by The Whisperer. The Whisperer's touch had left her feeling groped and unclean.

Her gaze turned to the tub. The need to wash off The Whisperer's touch overwhelmed her.

"Are you all right?" the man asked through the door.

"I'm fine. I'm going to bathe."

"I don't think you're steady enough yet."

"I'm going to bathe," she returned, her voice holding no compromise.

His silence gave away his reticence, but finally he said, "If you feel faint, yell."

Victoria remained sitting while she stripped. Once finished, she stared at the pile of discarded clothing. "I think I'll burn them." She was certain she recalled seeing her suitcases in the bedroom. If that had been merely wishful thinking, she would borrow something from her host, but she was never going to slip one toe into the clothes on the bathroom floor ever again.

Climbing into the tub, she drew the shower curtain and turned on the water. As the hot water cascaded over her, she was certain nothing had ever felt this good. Her legs were still weak and when she bent over to pick up the bottle of shampoo on the side of the tub, dizziness threatened to send her reeling. Sitting down under the flow of the water, she waited until the sensation had subsided, then lathered her hair.

Luxury. Absolute luxury. She issued a sigh of pure pleasure as she rinsed the suds out of her hair, then soaped her body.

Standing by the door, fresh towel in hand, listening for any sign of trouble from inside, Lance frowned more darkly at himself. If she required help, he needed to be there in an instant. *Time to bite the bullet.*

Opening the door, he entered the room. The shower curtain prevented him from seeing her, but the remembered feel of her in his arms gave his imagination fodder and he found himself visualizing her nude body, wet and sudsy. Fire ignited within him. *Erase that thought!* he ordered himself.

"Are you all right?" he demanded.

Startled by his voice, she scooted to the back of the tub and peered around the curtain. "What are you doing in here?"

Lance had never seen a woman look more desirable. It took a great deal of effort, but outwardly he maintained a cool, indifferent facade. "I figured that if you fainted, I wouldn't be much help in the hall," he said with staid formality, while inwardly he fought a bout of lust more powerful than any he'd ever experienced.

She let the shower curtain fall between them again, seemed to take a moment to rinse thoroughly, then reached her arm around the curtain. "May I have a towel?"

Lance placed the towel in her hand. In his mind's eye he visualized her first drying her hair, then rubbing down her body. His imagination was definitely working overtime. Anger that he was having so much trouble keeping his mind on the business at hand raged through him. This was not like him at all. Even in situations where he could not control all of the elements, he was always in total control of himself. Victoria Rockford was having a very disquieting effect on him.

"I'm certain I can make it back to the bedroom on my own," she said through the curtain.

Lance would have liked nothing better than to obey the dismissal in her voice. But he couldn't. "I'll just stick around and make sure you don't need a helping hand."

The towel securely in place, Victoria pulled back the curtain.

Lance felt numb. She was even sexier than he'd imagined. *Duty, man. Remember your duty,* he ordered himself. Stepping back, he gave her room to step out of the tub. When she teetered slightly, he caught her by the elbow. The contact sent a charged current of heat racing through him.

Acutely aware of his touch, Victoria was startled to realize that she had no desire to pull away. Instead, she liked the feel of his hand…it made her feel secure, safe. *He's allowed you to see him. If he's one of the bad guys, he's probably planning to kill you eventually!* she reminded herself and the safe feeling vanished.

When he released her quickly after they'd reached the hall, Victoria recognized that he'd held on to her for only as long as was absolutely necessary for her to regain her balance. Glancing toward him covertly, she saw his shuttered expression and her fear increased. On one hand, he was taking very good care of her. But on the other, his cold, impersonal behavior indicated that he did not consider her someone he wanted to befriend.

Able to make it back to the bedroom on her own, she entered and closed the door. Curiously, she missed her stoic companion's presence. *You really are muddled,* she mocked herself. She didn't even know if he was friend or foe. And right now, her money was on *foe.*

Chapter Two

Outside the bedroom door, Lance stood immobilized by indecision. He was not certain his control was strong enough, should he insist on helping Victoria dress. The effect she had on him was more than disturbing. It was unnerving.

Finally, deducing she was steady enough to find her own clothes and dress herself, he returned to the kitchen and finished warming up some soup. He carried it back to the bedroom and knocked before entering. Inside, he found her dressed in a fresh pair of slacks and a lightweight sweater, sitting in the chair he'd occupied earlier, combing her hair. She stopped and looked his way.

"Your soup," he said, extending the cup of hot liquid toward her. "I thought you should start with something light."

"Thank you," she said, accepting the cup.

Lance seated himself on the end of the bed and studied her. The sunlight shone on her hair, highlighting strands of gold among the dark brown tresses. His gaze traveled to her face. Even without makeup she was beautiful. *She's a Thorton, of royal blood, and a woman I am sworn to serve,* he reminded himself curtly.

Victoria was aware of his scrutiny as she sipped her soup. Looking at him, she said, "I would like to go home now."

"It's not safe for you to leave here just yet." He read the distrust in her eyes. The last thing he needed was for her to try to run away from him. "I assure you, my concern is only for your welfare. It is my duty to see that no harm comes to you."

"It is your *duty* to keep me safe from harm?"

Deciding she was not ready to hear the full truth just yet, he said simply, "Yes."

Victoria tried to remember what he'd told her in the cabin. The memory was too vague, too filled with shadowy images. "And who did you say you are?"

"I am Captain Lance Grayson, Head of the Investigative Division of the Royal Security Detail of Thortonburg. I was assigned to find you."

Victoria had to admit he did look like a protector. But she still wasn't ready to trust him. "Do you have some sort of identification?"

From his pocket, he produced a leather-encased gold badge.

It looked real, Victoria admitted. But it didn't make any sense that someone from the Royal Security Detail would be looking for her. Their duty was to protect the royal family. There were other agencies for commoners to turn to. "So you found me. Why can't you take me home?"

"Your kidnappers are still at large. It is possible they will worry that you can identify them. They might seek to eliminate you. For now, it's safest to keep you in hiding."

His reasoning sounded plausible. Maybe the royal security people were called in on kidnappings. Those were very rare occurrences in their little country. Enlightenment suddenly dawned on her. "It was a mistake, wasn't it? The kidnappers kidnapped the wrong person."

"It was no mistake."

She looked at him skeptically. "Then, do you know why I was kidnapped?"

"For ransom."

Her disbelief increased. "That doesn't make any sense. In the first place, my father isn't wealthy. He's a headmaster. And in the second place, anyone who knew anything about us would know he wouldn't pay even a wooden nickel to set me free." She flushed with embarrassment at having admitted to a stranger how strained her relationship with her father was, but her companion showed no surprise, only curiosity.

"To aid us in capturing the person or persons who abducted you, I need to know all you can remember about your kidnapping."

Victoria would have preferred to forget the whole ordeal, but she wanted The Whisperer caught and brought to justice. And, if Captain Grayson was on the level, he was certainly the man who could do just that. "I remember arriving in Thortonburg. I'd taken the bus from the airport. I got in late. Very late. I was walking to my flat, when I was grabbed from behind." She paused as a tremor of remembered fear shook her. "Something evil-smelling was pressed over my nose and mouth. I woke in the cabin, bound, gagged and blindfolded." Suddenly realizing she had no clue as to how long she'd been in captivity, she asked, "What is today's date?"

Lance told her.

"I was held for well over a week," she murmured, then added, "it felt more like a year."

Lance obviously sensed the strain that remembering was causing her because his tone softened to a gentle but firm coaxing. "What do you recall of your captivity?"

Again she found herself not wanting to remember. It was only Captain Grayson's presence that made her feel secure enough to allow her mind to go back to those dreadful days. He was, she thought, very like a granite pillar. For a moment she remained silent to allow the memories to become clearer, then she spoke again. "I remember that when I first woke, there were ropes binding my wrists. I had almost gotten them loose when The Whisperer arrived."

"The Whisperer?"

"That's the name I gave my captor because he always whispered." She shivered. "It was an ugly whisper. Malicious. I could swear I heard amusement in it as if he was enjoying himself immensely."

He won't enjoy himself when I catch up with him, Lance vowed. "You say you had almost freed yourself when he returned?"

Victoria nodded. "He said it was lucky for me he'd arrived when he did. He said that if I'd freed my hands and taken my blindfold off and seen him, he'd have to kill me. Then he said that would be a shame because he'd gone to so much trouble to see that he didn't have to go that far. He told me he'd waited to start giving me sedatives until the chloroform had worn off so that he could be certain not to use too many drugs on me at any one time. Then he said he'd have to use his handcuffs in the future."

"Do you remember anything that might identify the man you call The Whisperer?"

Victoria studied her proclaimed rescuer. Again, the thought played through her mind that if he was truly on her side, she had found a champion who could protect her. But nothing about what was happening to her made any sense. And the fact that he refused to take her home continued to feed her suspicions.

Then there was his very official, very stiff manner. On one hand, it was assuring. On the other, she would have felt more at ease if he'd behaved, at least a little, as if he wanted to be her friend. Until she found out what was really going on, she would trust no one. And as soon as the opportunity arose, she would escape and search out the truth on her own.

Turning her mind back to The Whisperer, Victoria concentrated hard for a long moment, then said, "No, nothing definitive. He came a couple of times a day, I think, and would unbind me, lead me to the facilities, let me use them, then have me drink down a can of something that tasted like a food supplement. Then he'd make me swallow more pills. The first couple of times, I tried not to swallow them, but he put a gun to my head and gave me no choice.' A shiver of disgust shook her. "Every time he came, I required more and more help from him." Not wanting to remember anymore, she turned her gaze to the window. "Since you will not take me home, will you at least allow me to go outside?"

"Yes, of course." He rose and took the mug from her, then offered her his arm.

Studying the holstered gun as she accepted his aid to rise, she wondered if she could extract it from the holster quicker than he could stop her. At the moment, she knew she couldn't, and without the gun she was no match for his strength. So for now she would continue to play his game, whatever that game was. Once on her feet, she released him. She could not shake the fear that he was the enemy and his sturdiness unnerved her. "I can walk on my own," she said.

Respectful of her wish, Lance stepped back and allowed her to proceed ahead of him.

Victoria moved slowly, not only because her body was still sluggish, but also because she wanted to survey her surroundings. The room across from the bedroom looked like a study. Pausing at the doorway, she asked, "Whose house is this?"

"Mine," Lance replied.

His answer was encouraging. Surely he would not have taken her to his place if he intended to harm her. It would be too difficult to get rid of all the evidence that she'd been there. Wondering if he would stop her, she entered the study, hoping to find clues that would tell her if her host was being honest with her.

Aware of the furtive glances she'd cast his way, Lance knew she still didn't trust him. He couldn't blame her. Her kidnapping had been a terrible ordeal. And, because she didn't know the whole truth, a confusing one. In her shoes, he wouldn't be ready to trust too quickly, either.

He was well aware of the strained relationship

between father and daughter, but for Victoria to suspect Malcolm Rockford wouldn't lift a finger, or spare a dime, to save her saddened him.

He found himself thinking that most men would believe she was worth much more than her weight in gold and jewels. There was an aura about her that lit up a room. The Grand Duke was certain to be pleased when she was presented to him.

Hoping that allowing her the freedom to explore his home would ease her distrust of him, he remained in the doorway, making no move to stop her.

She paused in front of a large, well-stocked bookcase. It contained everything from classics to the most current modern fiction. "Have you really read all of these books?"

"Yes."

Surprise registered on her face. She turned to him. "Really?"

"Yes."

"I'm impressed." She turned her attention to a wall with an assortment of photographs and plaques. The photographs were of him with Victor Thorton, Grand Duke of Thortonburg, and King Phillip of Wynborough, along with other members of their respective royal families. Inscriptions thanked him for his service. The plaques were special honors for bravery. There were also two glass shadow boxes with military medals, including two medals for valor. Clearly, she could see he was who he said he was.

She turned to him again. "You've had a very notable career."

The stoic mask he had trained himself to always keep in place remained unchanged, but the honest admiration in her voice caused a surge of pleasure deep within. *I'm merely relieved that she finally believes me,* he told himself. Aloud, he said, "I take my duty very seriously."

Victoria looked back at the photographs. His expression in each was the same one of cool command. Again, she turned back to him. "Do you ever smile?"

Lance knew others considered him a bit too grim, but he was comfortable with the path he'd chosen. Though many thought of him as cold and, perhaps, in some cases even unlikable, they always turned to him when they needed help. "Not when I'm on duty."

Victoria continued to study him. "Maybe your muscles are already frozen in that position and you can't smile." She gulped, as if normally she was a bit more prudent than that.

Lance found himself having to fight to keep the corners of his mouth from tilting upward. "That is possible."

Victoria saw the hint of amusement in his eyes. That he could laugh at himself made him seem a little less austere and certainly more human. In the next instant the amusement was gone, replaced by cool command. Clearly, he was intent on keeping any softer side of himself private. Heading to the door, she noticed that he stepped back immediately to allow her to exit.

"You have a very comfortable home," she said, as she glanced into the kitchen, then continued on into the living room. "Definitely on the masculine side, but nice."

Again Lance was surprised by how very pleased her approval made him. Long ago he'd stopped caring what other people thought and lived his life by his own personal code. "I hope that means you won't mind spending a few days here, if that proves necessary."

Victoria opened the French doors that led out onto a wide, screened-in porch facing the ocean. This was the kind of place she'd hoped to find for herself one day. But that was in the future. Right now she must deal with the present.

Although her body was still somewhat weak, the languid effect of the drugs on her mind had nearly worn off. At an early age, she had taken command of her life. It was time for her to take control again. "I hope you don't take this wrong. Your home is very pleasant, your view is magnificent and you've been very kind, but I have a life to get back to. I took a leave of absence from my job because I felt the need to get away for a time. My mother's death has been very difficult for me to accept. But I should be getting back before they decide to give my job to someone else."

"I have already explained that it is not yet safe for you to return home."

Again The Whisperer's hot, ugly breath blowing against her face came back to haunt her and terror curled through her. "When will it be safe?"

"Soon."

Victoria could not shake the feeling that he wasn't telling her everything. Stepping out onto the porch, she considered going down to the beach, but her legs were tiring. "What kind of drug did they give me? And when is it going to wear off?" she demanded in frustration, seating herself on the porch swing.

"I can't be certain what drug, exactly. Some sort of sedative," he replied. "The reason you're still sluggish is because of the cumulative effect and your forced inactivity. Being up and moving around should help you to improve fairly rapidly."

Even knowing her host was who he claimed to be, Victoria remained uneasy. Being kidnapped didn't make sense. Being rescued by royal commandos and then protected by such a high-ranking royal security person made even less sense. Looking up and down the beach, she saw no other houses. "Just exactly where are we?" Even as she asked, she wondered if he'd answer.

"We're about an hour and a half southwest of Thortonburg."

Alarms sounded in her mind. "That's a bit far for you to commute, isn't it?"

"I have quarters in the castle. This is my private retreat."

That was plausible, she conceded. Still, as her gaze again swept the beach in both directions and she saw no signs that anyone else was near, her uneasiness increased. "Definitely private."

"The thirty acres to the north belong to Sir Ralph Bryce. The twenty acres to the south belong to Charles Howser, the wealthy industrialist. Both like their privacy, so they have built their homes at quite a distance apart."

Victoria knew the men from articles written about them in the tabloids. Both traveled extensively, causing her to guess they were rarely at their beach homes. If she did discover she needed to escape, she probably couldn't count on finding one of them at home to aid her. "So just how long do you predict I will have to stay here?"

"The ransom is scheduled to be paid tomorrow morning in a park in the Mulberry neighborhood of Thortonburg. With luck, your captor will either return to the cabin and be caught there, or he'll be captured when he attempts to pick up the ransom."

"My father actually came through with the ransom?" she asked incredulously.

"Yes. But, since you have been freed, we'll be putting out a decoy rather than the real money."

Victoria hardly noticed what he said. She was still reeling from the knowledge that Malcolm had been willing to pay her ransom. "I still can't believe Father came up with the money. If it had been my sister, Rachel, I could understand. He always favored her. But he treated me like dirt under his boot." The thought that the threat of her death had made Malcolm realize he did care for her brought a rush of joy. For most of her life she'd told herself she didn't care what he thought. Now she admitted that she had wanted him to care for her. He was, after all, her father. "I should call him."

When she started to rise, Lance moved into a position that blocked her entrance into the house. "That wouldn't be wise."

Immediately, Victoria was on her guard. Maybe her host was a good guy turned bad. But that didn't make any sense. If he'd wanted to kidnap someone for ransom, surely he would have chosen one of the royals. He certainly had easy access to them. "Why can't I call my father?"

Lance had been prepared for this. "His phone might be bugged and we don't want the kidnappers to know you're free."

"Surely you would know if it was bugged or not."

She looked like a filly ready to bolt. Lance didn't like being the one to deliver the news, but the time had come to tell her the truth. "There are things you need to know."

His words carried an ominous ring. Meeting his gaze, Victoria saw uneasiness in the gray depths of his eyes. Clearly he was worried about how she would take whatever it was he had to tell her. Her body stiffened as she braced herself. "What do I need to know?"

"There is no easy way to say this." Lance paused.

He's going to tell me that he's part of the kidnapping plot and has to kill me! Victoria's hands balled into fists. She would not go down without a fight. "Just say it," she demanded through clenched teeth.

"Malcolm Rockford is not your father."

Victoria sat starting at him dumbly. If she'd made a list of a hundred things he might tell her, that revelation would not even have entered her mind. "That's absurd."

Lance saw the shock on her face and took a step toward her in order to catch her if she should faint. As he drew nearer, the desire to take her hands in his as an offer of support was strong. Telling himself it would not be proper, he held himself back. Deep within, he was forced to admit there was another reason he wanted to avoid any contact. Just looking at her had a disquieting effect on him. Touching her threatened to crack the shield he kept around his emotions and that was something he would not allow. "It is the truth."

"Are you telling me that I was one of those babies who was accidentally switched at birth in the hospital?"

"No." Lance had thought that once he got the

first part out, the rest would be easy. It wasn't. If
she had idolized her mother, what he had to tell her
next could be an even greater blow.

"I was adopted?"

"No."

Victoria stared at him in silence for a long moment, then said stiffly, "For as long as I can remember, I have always known that I was born sooner
than nine months after my parents were married. My
mother said I was premature, but my birth weight
was nearly the same as my sister's and she was full-
term. I always suspected that my mother was pregnant when she married Malcolm Rockford, but I assumed he was my father."

"Your mother was pregnant when she married,
but Rockford wasn't the father." Lance took another
step closer, her paleness increasing his worry that
she might faint.

Victoria drew in a deep breath. Leaning back in
the swing, she lifted her legs upward and wrapped
her arms around them. Sitting with her chin resting
on her knees, she stared out at the ocean.

Recognizing her need for silence, Lance eased
himself into a nearby chair. The lost look on her
face tore at him. For her sake, he wished the worst
of her shock was over, but he knew it wasn't. Knowing that once she absorbed what he'd told her there
would be more questions, he sat tensely, like a man
waiting for the second shoe to fall and wishing he
could make this easier for her.

Hell, if she'd had my parents for a mother and father, she'd be rejoicing right now, Lance mused bitterly. Immediately, he scowled at himself. He thought he'd put his anger behind him. It served no purpose.

Victoria's childhood played through her mind. Memories so hurtful she'd tried to erase them came flooding back. "I used to think there was something terribly wrong with me because my own father couldn't love me. I remember when I was in third grade. I got the lead part in this little production the teachers decided to put on. I worked so hard to be perfect. The audience was effusive. Of course, I know now that we could have all stumbled over our feet and forgotten all our lines and they would have cheered. That's what parents do.

"Anyway, I was basking in the glow of success. But on the way home, Father...Malcolm started telling me all the things I'd done wrong. I was crying by the time we reached the house. My mother admonished him, saying I was just a child and she thought I'd done very well. Malcolm gave her one of his superior looks and said that people should tell the truth, no matter how unsavory."

This was one of those images that had remained sharp, no matter how hard she'd tried to erase the memory. Now, in her mind's eye, she saw her mother's and Malcolm's faces. Her mother had looked stricken and clamped her mouth shut, saying no more. Malcolm had looked pleased with himself.

As the full impact of that exchange hit her, she said in a voice barely above a whisper, "He was chiding my mother for lying to him. He must have known or, at least, suspected all along that I was not his."

"It is my duty to see that he causes you no further harm."

His words only half sank in as more memories of her youth continued to flow. She could not count the number of times her mother had told her not to pay any heed to Malcolm's criticisms. Maribelle Rockford had explained that her husband was a perfectionist and no one could live up to his standards. But Victoria had noticed that, her sister, Rachel, had garnered Malcolm's praise. And he had been jealously possessive of Maribelle. Only Victoria had been made to feel like an unwanted intruder in his household.

Refusing to allow the hurtful memories to overwhelm her, she rested her forehead on her knees and forcefully shoved the images from her mind.

"Would you like some coffee?" Lance offered, feeling the need to provide what comfort he could. Anger toward the cruelty she'd suffered under Malcolm's rule raged through him. Like him, she'd had no choice regarding the circumstances of her birth, and yet she'd been the one to pay the price.

Lifting her head, Victoria again stared at the sea. A shiver shook her. She was not certain if she was really cold or if it was shock that chilled her. Her mother's death and now the discovery that she wasn't who she thought she was made rational thinking difficult. Unable to even speak, she simply nodded her acceptance of his offer.

Lance regarded her with concern as he rose. Seeing her shiver, he retrieved his jacket from a peg on the wall. "Cream or sugar or both?" he asked as he wrapped the jacket around her shoulders.

His fingers brushing against her sent jolts of heat coursing through Victoria. It was as if his touch fed strength into her. Her gaze traveled upward over his broad chest to his face. In spite of the cold, stern set of his jaw, he made her feel safe and secure. "Neither, thank you."

Lance saw the lingering pain in her eyes and the desire to take her in his arms and kiss her sadness away became strong. In the next instant, that desire was erased by self-directed anger. Years ago, he'd banished those kind of tender emotions forever. And yet, from the moment he'd first seen her picture he'd sensed those emotions trying to find new life. That was something he would never allow. *In the future, remember to keep your distance,* he ordered himself, quickly stepping back. "I'll get that coffee."

As he disappeared into the house, Victoria found herself missing his company. That was not like her. She prided herself on her ability to stand alone, needing no one. Even more surprising was that she should feel so drawn to this man she barely knew. Normally, she was very hesitant when it came to forming alliances.

Taking in a deep breath of the fresh ocean breeze, she suddenly froze, locking the air in her lungs. Captain Grayson said her father had come up with the ransom. If Malcolm wasn't her father, who was? Releasing the breath, she rose and went inside. She met the captain in the living room on his way to the porch, coffee mugs in hand. "Who is my father?"

For a moment he hesitated, then said, "Victor Thorton, Grand Duke of Thortonburg."

She didn't care how many photographs the man had with himself and various dignitaries. He was obviously a nutcase. "That's ridiculous. My mother and the Grand Duke? No way." Realizing his hands were occupied with the coffee cups, Victoria made a grab for the gun. Lance cursed under his breath as she snapped the holster open and extracted the weapon.

Stepping back, holding the gun on him, Victoria frowned. "That was way too easy. Are there really bullets in this thing?"

"Yes, there are bullets," he replied, setting aside the coffee cups. "I didn't want you to get burned with the coffee. I gave your father my word, I would protect you from harm."

His voice carried the ring of truth, but Victoria refused to be swayed. She was well aware that some sick minds could even fool lie detector machines. "You were just worried that if you tried to stop me, I would accidentally shoot you. Now get your hands up."

"Women," Lance muttered. Reaching across the space between them, his hand closed over the gun. "Give me back my weapon."

Victoria ordered herself to pull the trigger. She couldn't. Where his fingers touched hers a heat radiated through her, paralyzing her into inaction. Tears of frustration welled in her eyes as she released her hold.

Lance couldn't believe he'd allowed her to get his gun. Normally he was much more alert. She was having a very disconcerting effect on him. That body, that face, those blue eyes, that long dark hair…she'd have a disconcerting effect on any man, he reasoned. What shocked him was that he wasn't angry with her. In fact, he again found himself admiring her spunk. Seeing the tears in her eyes, he attempted to soothe her as he reholstered the gun. "You couldn't have fired anyway. The safety was on."

"If that's supposed to make me feel better, it doesn't," she growled back. "My one chance to escape from whatever game you're playing and I blew it."

His gaze bore into hers, willing her to believe him. "I am not playing a game."

"All right, for argument's sake, let's say you aren't a lunatic and this isn't a game. So how long has the Grand Duke known about me? All my life?"

Mentally, Lance grinned. In the photograph the kidnappers had sent to prove Victoria was still alive, he'd seen fire and a touch of devilry in her features. That she wasn't afraid to admit that she thought he might be a lunatic showed a depth of spirit that went even deeper than he'd imagined. He was well aware that most people who knew him would have been much too intimidated to have made such a statement to his face. "No. He learned about you when the ransom note arrived."

Her skepticism returned full force. "So all you have is some kidnapper's word that I'm the Grand Duke's daughter? And you want me to believe that the Grand Duke confessed to having a liaison with my mother and claimed me as his daughter?"

"It didn't happen exactly that way."

Folding her arms in front of her, she stared hard into his face. "So how did it happen?"

For one brief second, Lance found himself so fascinated by the color of her eyes that he could think of nothing else. Silently admonishing himself for these moments of weakness, he said, "The Grand Duke received a ransom note with your picture enclosed. Anyone could see you were a Thorton. You have the same cheekbones, the nose, the eyes. The lips are a little fuller." *Kissably fuller.* Lance glowered. Duty alone should have prevented him from having thoughts like that about this woman.

"The world is full of look-alikes. I find it impossible to believe the Grand Duke would accept me as his daughter on the evidence of a photograph."

"There was also a description of a birthmark.

You have a raspberry teardrop on your left hip, right?"

"Yes." Victoria flushed scarlet at his intimate knowledge of her body.

Lance attempted to pose his next question with as much finesse as possible. "How many people know about your birthmark?"

"My mother knew, but she's deceased. That leaves my fa…" She stopped and corrected herself. "Malcolm. My sister. My doctor. His nurse." Victoria paused, obviously thinking hard. "I can't think of anyone else."

"No boyfriends who might have taken a peek?" Lance persisted. His words tasted acid on his tongue and he realized he hated the idea that she might have been with another man. In the next instant, he was mocking himself. She would never be his. That the notion had even been a shadow in his mind was absurd.

Victoria's chin tightened with defiance. "I suppose you'll think I'm archaic, but no. I was saving myself for marriage." The truth was, she'd never met a man who aroused her enough to make her want to give up her virginity. Abruptly she recalled the currents of heat any contact with the stoic Captain Grayson caused to flow through her. *This whole situation has me hypersensitive,* she reasoned. Shaken that even a momentary romantic thought had crossed her mind, she broke eye contact with him. She was looking for a man who was sensitive, warm and tender. Captain Grayson didn't fit that picture the least little bit.

Lance was pleased with her answer, much too pleased. Her love life, he admonished himself again, was not his concern. However, the fact that she had no lovers did narrow the field of suspects dramatically. "Have you ever been hospitalized?"

"No." Looking very tired, Victoria rounded the couch and sat down. She rested her head in her hands. "I still can't believe any of this."

Knowing she needed time to assimilate what she'd learned, Lance decided to change the subject. "The coffee's a little cool. I'll get you a fresh cup."

Victoria merely nodded. When the captain returned with her coffee, she accepted the cup with murmured thanks and tried to concentrate only on the hot liquid.

Seating himself in a nearby chair, Lance studied her worriedly. The silence that filled the room was tense. She had been through a tremendous emotional turmoil already and, if his suspicions were true, she had more ahead. Until this moment he had dealt with whatever pain life handed him and others with stoic acceptance. People either toughened up or crumbled. In his view, that was the way of the world. But with all his being, he wished he could soften the blows life was dealing this woman.

Finished with her coffee, Victoria curled up on the couch and slept.

Spreading a blanket over her to keep her from

getting chilled, Lance could not resist gently combing her hair away from her face with his fingers. Her skin was soft and enticing.

Hands off! he ordered himself and stepped away.

Chapter Three

Victoria awoke slowly. For a few moments she was disoriented, uncertain of where she was. But she was not frightened. She felt safe and secure. Her gaze first focused on the fire burning in the hearth. She shifted her head and a pair of long legs came into view. A curl of delight wove through her. *Captain Lance Grayson, Head of the Investigative Division of the Royal Security Detail.* My hero.

He was definitely hero material...tall, dark, ruggedly handsome and strongly built. But not a Prince Charming, she noted, adding "cold as an iceberg and stern as granite" to her list of adjectives. Still, she was very glad to have him with her.

Noticing her attempt to shift into a sitting position, Lance put aside the book he'd been reading. "How do you feel?"

"Hungry." The word was out before she even realized how ravenous she was.

"I'll make you a sandwich. I hope roast beef is all right with you. Mustard or mayonnaise? Lettuce?"

She searched for any friendliness in his face or voice. She saw and heard only polite deference. Clearly she was nothing more than a duty to him. Well, so be it. He'd rescued her from that horrible cabin and that was all that mattered. She did not require his friendship. "Mayonnaise and lettuce, please."

When he left for the kitchen, she rose and headed to the bathroom. To her delight, her legs—her whole body, in fact—responded normally, her sluggishness gone. Her sandwich and a cup of coffee were waiting for her on the coffee table when she returned. Ravenous, she concentrated on eating.

"Would you like another?" Lance offered, noting how quickly she'd consumed her food.

"No, thanks." Victoria took a long sip of the coffee and stared into the fire. Questions again assailed her. "You said the ransom note did not contain my name. How did you know to look for *me?*"

"Luckily the Grand Duke is not a philanderer. He remembered your mother's name—at least, her first name. When we presented him with information on Maribelle Leighton, he confirmed that she'd been his lover. His liaison with Maribelle was the only time he was unfaithful. He and the Duchess were having trouble at the time, and separated for a short while.''

''I suppose, if she can hear us, she'll be happy to know she had some lasting effect on him. He certainly had one on her,'' Victoria commented dryly.

''I would say that he must have thought highly of her to have remembered her name after twenty-eight years.'' *And her daughter would have the same lasting effect on any man,* Lance grudgingly realized. He'd tried to ignore her while she slept, but had found himself constantly glancing her way.

''I suppose,'' Victoria conceded. ''I know I keep saying this, but I truly find all of this hard to believe. Of course it does explain some things my mother used to say to me. She was always admonishing me to behave prudently and warning me that if I did not, I could live to regret it.'' A deep sadness for Maribelle Rockford filled her. ''I realize now she was talking about herself.'' Pushing the painful memories of her mother to the back of her mind, she concentrated on Captain Grayson. ''You were telling me how you found me.''

''Although we confirmed your mother was the Grand Duke's lover and that she had given birth within the time frame that would make you the Grand Duke's daughter, our only problem was not knowing where to concentrate our search. Though we knew you'd arrived in Thortonburg safely, there was no telling where in the Grand Duchy the kidnappers held you. Our big break came when Prince

Damon Montague and your sister contacted me about a possible location.''

Confusion again threatened to overwhelm Victoria. ''Rachel contacted you? But she's living out of the country. How would she know to contact you? And how did Prince Damon get into the picture?''

''Your sister became worried when she couldn't reach you. She said she was certain something was wrong so she returned to Thortonburg to find you. The prince met her at the Thortonburg police precinct and got involved in the search with her. He was aware we were looking for the Grand Duke's missing daughter, saw your picture, saw the resemblance to the Thortons, was certain you were the one we were looking for and eventually he and Rachel contacted the Thortons.''

The omission of one person from Captain Grayson's narrative was causing her stomach to knot. ''You have said nothing of my fa...of Malcolm Rockford. Wasn't he concerned when I didn't return home?''

''At first he told your friend, Heidi, that you'd called and informed him you were extending your vacation on the continent. Then he told your sister that he knew you'd made it back to Thortonburg, but that you'd told him you were going to visit a friend on your return.''

''None of that's true.'' She didn't want to acknowledge what she was thinking. It was too horrible a suspicion. "I suppose one of the kidnappers must have called him and pretended to be me."

"That's possible."

Victoria heard the doubt in his voice. Surprised he had not bluntly told her what he really thought, she realized he was trying to alleviate any further shock by giving her the opportunity to adjust to the truth at her own speed. Captain Lance Grayson was much more sensitive than his outward demeanor suggested.

Victoria's mind flashed to the cabin that had been her prison. Memories of fishing and hunting trips Malcolm had gone on when she was a child came sharply back. He'd gone alone or with his uncle— her great-uncle on her father's side. Victoria had loved those weekends with just her, her mother and Rachel at home. And there had even been some weekends when Malcolm had taken Rachel along, leaving just her and her mother. Usually, memories of those precious times made her glad. Now she didn't want to believe the cabin where she'd been held captive was the same as the one he'd used for his retreats. Barely able to say the words, she asked, "The cabin where you found me...how did you know to look there, at that particular cabin? There must be hundreds of old abandoned houses or places a person could be hidden."

"Your sister recalled a cabin her father once took her to. She remembered what river it was on and said she thought it belonged to a great-uncle who had moved to Australia several years ago."

For a long moment Victoria was silent, then stiffly she said, "Rachel believes Fa…" Again she stopped herself from referring to Malcolm as Father. Just the thought left a bitter taste on her tongue. "Rachel believes Malcolm was involved?"

"She was concerned that he was taking your disappearance too lightly. And she was aware of the strain that has always existed between you and him."

Victoria's hands balled into fists as she fought to control the mix of emotions boiling within her. "I have always suspected that he didn't love me, but to do this…" Her cheeks flushed red with the anger and hurt she'd suppressed for so many years. "Do you have any idea how it makes a child feel when they're rejected by a parent?"

Memories Lance kept locked away in the deep recesses of his mind burst free to haunt him. He shoved them back.

"I once told my mother that I didn't think Malcolm liked me. She said that he simply wasn't a demonstrative man. But I saw the way he was with Rachel. He showed a warmth toward her. There was never any warmth in his eyes when he looked at me." Victoria's jaw tensed as she fought to hold back tears. "But I never thought he hated me so much, he would actually harm me."

There was no doubt in Lance's mind that Rockford had planned to kill her. Her description of the cabin would have led him right to the man. And it wasn't his nature to hedge on the truth in a situation like this simply to spare a person's feelings, but he understood her pain and could not stop himself from trying to ease it. "I'm sure that if he was involved, he meant to release you without injury."

Her jaw trembled. "After my mother's death, I thought Malcolm was actually warming up to me. For the first time in my life, he took an interest in me. I figured that was because he was alone... Rachel had expressed no intention of returning home. That just left him and me." Bitterness laced her voice. "He even gave me money for my trip so that I could be away longer. He said he knew how much I was grieving over my mother and that a change in environment would do me good."

As the impact of her words hit Lance full-force, rage spread through him. "He was trying to keep you out of the way until the ransom was paid."

In his mind's eye, Lance visualized her lying bound, gagged, blindfolded and drugged on the cot in the cabin. If she had died, her blood would have been on his hands. The intensity of this realization caused the barrier he kept around his emotions to break. In one lithe movement, he left his chair, knelt on one knee before her and took her hands in his. "I am so sorry for what's happened to you. I would rather lose my right arm than see the pain Malcolm Rockford has inflicted upon you." The words tore from deep within the core of his being…a core he had spent a lifetime keeping secret and untouched by others.

The sincerity and self-admonishment in his voice caused Victoria's heart to skip a beat. His hands encased hers in a protective warmth that spread through her like wildfire. Looking into his eyes, she saw a depth of tenderness she would never have imagined him capable of. This Captain Grayson moved her as no man had ever moved her. The suffering she'd experienced in the cabin became minor to the need to alleviate any guilt he felt for not rescuing her sooner. "You found me in time, Captain Grayson. For that I will always be grateful."

His hold on her hands tightened. "I promise you that I will not allow any further harm to come to you."

Victoria felt as if she was caught up in a fantasy…a daydream with a knight in shining armor kneeling at her feet and pledging himself to her. It was the most delightful sensation. "There is no one whose hands I would feel safer placing my life in."

The effect she had on him was too strong. It was unlike anything he'd ever experienced before.

Suddenly embarrassment flowed through him. He had not behaved so openly since he was six years old. He wondered how she would react if he told her his life story beginning with his birth in a filthy room in a condemned building in the worst slum in Thortonburg. But his past was his own private hell, not to be shared with anyone, especially a princess. Displeased to have allowed his emotions to momentarily rule, he forced them behind their protective wall, released his hold, stood and bowed. "You are most gracious, Your Highness."

Victoria was not certain which startled her more…Captain Grayson's instant transformation back to his cool, stoic self or his reference to her as "Your Highness." Watching in silence as he returned to his chair, she wondered about the man beneath the staid mask he wore for the world. The desire to know more about that man grew stronger with each heartbeat. "So how did you come to be Head of the Investigative Division of the Royal Security Detail?"

"I achieved my rank by doing my duty, and right now my duty is to concentrate on capturing your kidnappers," he replied.

Victoria knew that she was being politely told that he didn't want to talk about himself. But the same spirit that had kept her from wilting under Malcolm's rule kept her from being intimidated into silence. "I would greatly enjoy a change in the subject of our conversation, at least for a while. Besides, it's only fair. You know a great deal about me, so I should know something about you. That's how acquaintanceships grow into friendships."

"As an employee of the Grand Duke, I am your faithful servant, Princess. That is as far as our acquaintanceship can ever *grow*."

Victoria frowned at this deferential, but unmistakable rebuke. Captain Lance Grayson clearly did not want to be her friend. Again she recalled the depth of tenderness she'd seen in his eyes. Had she imagined it? Or maybe she had just read too much into it. Maybe he was simply upset because he felt he'd been delinquent in his duty. He was definitely very big on duty. One thing she knew she hadn't imagined was that twice now he'd referred to her with a royal title. "I don't think there is any need for you to address me as if I'm a true royal. I'm not exactly legitimate."

"The Grand Duke intends to officially acknowledge you as his daughter."

Victoria stared at him in disbelief. "You can't be serious." The moment these words were out, she mocked herself for saying them. Of course, he was serious. She didn't know much about Captain Grayson, but the one thing she did know was that he didn't jest.

"When we're sure you're safe, he will present you publicly to his court, then to the country. The documents needed to have you legally become a Thorton have already been drawn up and require only your signature to make them complete. Once you have signed them, you will be Princess Victoria of Thortonburg."

A princess. A real princess. A thrill wove through her. In the next instant it was vanquished by reality. She could easily visualize the headlines in the tabloids…Grand Duke's Youthful Exploits Come Back To Haunt Him or For A Roll In The Hay Even The Grand Duke Must Pay. "What about all the gossip that will ensue? The Grand Duke is willing to subject himself and his family to that?"

"They're used to being gossiped about. That's part of public life."

Victoria regarded him dryly. "His claiming me is going to be a great deal more embarrassing than his falling off a horse during a polo match or the Grand Duchess wearing a dress that isn't becoming."

"The Grand Duke and Duchess are well-liked. They have accepted you and so will the rest of the country."

A casual observer would have noticed no difference in Captain Grayson's demeanor, but Victoria was no longer a casual observer. The warm depths of his eyes continued to haunt her, and she was determined to discover if it was her imagination or if the man she thought she'd seen did exist beneath the captain's armored exterior. And, because she was studying him so closely, she saw the slight twitch as his jaw tensed a fraction more than normal. "I don't think you are being entirely honest with me."

"Predictions, to be of any value, must be made on all of the facts." He paused. "During our search for you, we found nothing in your past that could be a source of gossip. However, if there is anything you feel could be embarrassing to you or the royal family, it would be best if you told me now."

"Other than being illegitimate and having the man I thought was my father kidnap me for a ransom, no, I can't think of anything in my life that could be uncomfortably embarrassing," Victoria returned dryly.

This display of cynical humor at her situation pleased Lance. It was more proof that she was strong enough to weather any storms ahead. "Those occurrences cannot be laid at your feet. You are the victim and the public will sympathize with you. As long as you don't do anything once you're brought into the fold to give people cause to gossip, the whispers will fade into nothingness."

Victoria gave him a wry look. "And so I get to be a royal princess, but I must live in a house of glass." Her expression hardened. "All my life, I've felt as if I've been living in a house of glass with Malcolm staring in the window and criticizing every move I make. Now I will have a nation doing it. I'm not so certain that even being a princess will be worth that price."

"You will have the support and protection of the royal family." *And mine, as well,* Lance heard himself adding silently. It bothered him that she had become so important to him. *It is my duty to oversee the safety of all members of the royal family. I am merely vowing to do my job,* he told himself.

Victoria continued to regard him dryly. "I find it very difficult to believe that the royal family is truly pleased to have me as its newest member."

"The Grand Duke is an honorable man. You have been done a dishonor by him, and he wishes to correct that. As for the Duchess, she is a good-hearted woman who wishes to see that the right thing is done by you. The princes, too, wish to see that the wrong is made right."

"In other words, they are accepting me because it is their duty as they see it."

"Duty is an honorable ethic."

Victoria frowned. "It may be an honorable ethic, but it's rather a cold one."

"It's dependable. You can always count on those who feel bound by it."

Victoria sighed. "I suppose you're right, but I prefer love and affection. Of course, I realize that isn't reasonable under the circumstances. But perhaps they might develop over time."

"Love and affection are fickle emotions. They cannot be counted on."

"You sound like a man who has loved and lost and is still bitter."

"I have never been and never intend to fall in love. That's a game for fools." As he spoke, he realized he was saying this as much to himself as to her. He had allowed her to break through the wall he kept around the emotions he'd vowed never to succumb to. He would not do that again. Choosing to end this conversation, he rose. "I need to check with my men to see if anyone's been to the cabin.

And I want to make certain their plans for the ransom drop are going well.''

Watching him depart, Victoria found herself even more intrigued by Captain Lance Grayson. What made him so cynical? Probably a woman, she decided, and he was just too proud to admit it. Something that felt like envy toward the woman who had been able to touch him so deeply wove through her. She frowned at herself. Right now, she had more important matters to concern herself with than the stoic Captain Grayson. Even with all the evidence that pointed in Malcolm's direction and the dislike she'd sensed from him all her life, she still did not want to believe he could be involved in her kidnapping.

And then there was the royal family. In spite of Captain Grayson's assurance that they were prepared to accept her, she wondered if it would merely be surface acceptance…that there would be an undercurrent of hostility. If so, she would be stepping into the same sort of environment she'd survived as a child. She would not willingly live under those conditions again.

''So what do I do?'' she muttered aloud. Her jaw firmed. She had remained in Thortonburg and subjected herself to Malcolm's tyranny because she had known her mother needed her. But she would never again subject herself to such meanness. If she felt unwelcome in the Grand Duke's household, she would pack her bags and leave.

Having made this decision, she spent the remainder of the day resting and regaining her strength. By the time she went to bed, she felt she had again claimed control of her future.

Victoria was awakened by the sound of her own scream. Her whole body was trembling with panic, and for a moment she wasn't certain what was real and what wasn't.

Even before she realized she'd merely been dreaming, the door of the room burst open. The light was flipped on, revealing Captain Grayson, gun in hand, scanning the room. "What's wrong?" he demanded harshly when he saw nothing.

Finding her voice, she said, "It was just a nightmare." As she spoke, the images again raced through her mind and it occurred to her that *nightmare* was an anemic description. She'd dreamed that she was back in the cabin. Captain Grayson had come to rescue her, but The Whisperer had jumped out of the shadows and delivered a deathblow to him. Grief for Captain Grayson had overwhelmed her.

"You're safe here. There is no need for you to be afraid."

Just hearing him tell her that she was safe had a soothing effect. Her fear subsiding, Victoria gazed at the man in front of her. His insistence that their relationship remain on the "barely acquainted" level made it clear that he didn't even want to be a friend and yet she had been devastated by his death. *He rescued me. It's only natural I would not want to see him harmed,* she reasoned. "I'm all right now," she assured him. "I'm sorry I disturbed you."

Lance nodded and left.

Victoria frowned as the door closed behind him and she recalled their argument earlier in the evening about sleeping arrangements. Now that she was feeling much better, she hadn't wanted to take his bed, but he had declared that she was the princess and he was her protector and that it was only right and proper for her to have the bedroom. The set of his jaw had convinced her that she had no chance of winning the debate. In the end, she'd thanked him graciously.

As for him, she knew he'd settled on the couch, taking off only his shoes so that he would be prepared for action should there be danger. He was obviously a man completely devoted to his duty. As this thought played through her mind, her mouth formed a pout and she recalled their discussion about love.

If he had been in love once, he would have been totally devoted to the woman. That, she felt certain, was his way. When the woman fell out of love, it would have been a crushing blow. That would explain his cynicism.

On the other hand, he'd said that he'd never been in love. Her first reaction had been to doubt his declaration. But on second thought, although other men might lie to save face, Captain Grayson didn't strike her as that kind of man. He'd said he'd never been in love and her tendency was to believe him. So why was he so dead set against it?

"Captain Lance Grayson should be the last thing on your mind," she admonished herself. He didn't even want to be her friend. Telling herself that her interest in him was merely a diversion from more serious matters she didn't want to think about at the moment, she curled up under the covers once again and went back to sleep.

In the living room, Lance lay staring at the ceiling. Never had he seen a woman look more enticing than Victoria had in his bed. He would never be so foolish as to allow himself to be in love with her, but he was in lust. That he could no longer deny. However, loyalty and duty to the Grand Duke forbade him to act on such feelings.

He had thought he would remain in service to the Grand Duke for the rest of his career. Now he was feeling restless. When this job was done, he would move on. He was bored, he told himself. But a tiny voice inside accused him of lying. It suggested he was running away from Victoria Rockford, that he was afraid she'd succeed in demolishing the stone wall he maintained around his heart.

He rolled over on the sofa and ignored the voice.

Chapter Four

"So what happened?" Victoria demanded as Lance hung up the phone. It was mid-morning and the ransom was to have been paid two hours earlier.

"No one came. Neither Malcolm nor his accomplice returned to the cabin in Glenshire, nor did they pick up the ransom in Thortonburg." Outwardly, Lance maintained an air of cool command. Inwardly, he was experiencing a growing uneasiness. That the kidnappers hadn't returned to the cabin hadn't set off any alarms. They could have decided that it was no longer necessary to tend to their captive. But that they hadn't shown up to collect the ransom suggested they could be aware Miss Rockford had been rescued and that the drop was a trap. In which case, they had to have knowledge of Lance and his men's movements.

On the other hand, it was possible that the kidnappers had simply gotten cold feet and decided to abandon the whole game. He couldn't be sure. The only thing he knew for certain was that they were still at large.

At least he had this cottage to hide her in. He knew they hadn't been followed here, and he'd been very careful to keep this place his secret.

"So what now?" Victoria prodded when he remained silent.

"Now we pick up Malcolm and question him. I didn't want to pick him up earlier because I didn't want him to know for certain we suspected him. And I was hoping he would show up at the cabin or the ransom drop so we would have solid proof against him." Reaching for the phone, Lance punched in a number and issued the order.

Victoria paced the floor, her anger bubbling to the surface once again. "I spent my youth trying to please that man, trying to make him like me."

Lance felt her words threatening to spark an old rage to life. "Dwelling on the past, on things that can never be changed, will do no good," he said as much to himself as to her. Shoving the rage back into its icy grave, he ordered himself to concentrate on the present.

"You're right." Victoria sighed and kept pacing. Memories of her nightmare taunted her. Something about The Whisperer nagged at her. When she had told Captain Grayson of her capture and her captivity, she had not been able to bring herself to concentrate on her captor. Now she did. "Malcolm wasn't The Whisperer," she announced abruptly. "If he is involved, he wasn't the one who did the dirty work."

"You've remembered something?"

"The Whisperer was shorter than Malcolm and heavier. I'm certain of that." Silently she cursed her lack of courage. "When I used the facilities, I was allowed to take my blindfold off so that I could see what I was doing. But he always warned me that he'd have to kill me if I didn't put it back on properly before he opened the door to let me out. I believed him, so I did." Her jaw tensed with self-directed anger. "I wish I'd had the nerve to peek just a little."

"You did the right thing."

"I suppose," Victoria conceded. Still, she was not happy with herself. Fighting the part of her that didn't want to remember any of her contact with her captor, she forced herself to try to recall something that would be useful. Triumph welled in her. "He wore a large ring on his right hand. I felt it when he pulled me to my feet. And he smelled of cigarettes."

"That could help." Lance read the strain on her face and knew how much it had cost her to force herself to concentrate on her captor. Again, he found himself admiring her toughness. "Can you think of any friends of Malcolm's who might fit that description.''

Victoria smiled dryly. "*Friends* and *Malcolm* are not two words I would normally put in the same sentence. He enjoyed spotting other people's faults and weaknesses and commenting on them. Of course, that was done behind their backs so they were unaware of how he really felt about them. I suppose there are those who would count themselves his friends, but in my opinion, he merely associated with them for his own personal amusement.''

"There was no one he shared confidences with?" Lance prodded. "No one he would trust if he needed someone to aid him in your kidnapping?"

Victoria shook her head. "Not that I can think of. He's not a trusting man and he truly believes he's a cut above everyone else. It's my opinion that he's tolerated, even treated with respect, because he's the headmaster at Thortonburg Academy and people feel he has their children's futures in his hands. But as for anyone being so good a friend they would aid him in such an endeavor, I can't name one. Trying to name someone I would even consider Malcolm's real friend is difficult enough. Of course, I've never really been privy to his private life outside of the house.''

"You can't think of anyone you would name as his friend?"

Victoria's nose wrinkled in distaste. "There is Lloyd Crenshaw, but he's a policeman and very cocky about that fact, too. He struts around as if being a lawman makes him better than others. The truth is, I can't abide him.''

"Your sister mentioned him as a friend of Malcolm's, as well. I've had him checked out, but so far nothing's turned up."

Victoria felt as if the walls were closing in on her. "I'd like to go for a walk on the beach," she announced and headed for the French doors.

Lance followed.

Outside, she breathed in the fresh, salty air and pushed thoughts of The Whisperer to the back recesses of her mind. She would try to think of something else useful later. Right now she needed a break. Pausing on the porch, she discarded her shoes, waited a moment longer for Captain Grayson to discard his, then headed out over the low dunes to the beach.

"It's very beautiful here," she said as she reached the edge of the water and stood gazing out at the waves rolling toward shore.

"Yes, it is." Lance had always found peace here, but standing with her beside him, he felt even more. It was as if she made the whole picture complete. *I do not need anyone but myself to make my world complete,* he snarled at himself. His mind went back to when he was six. Images branded into his brain helped him add another layer of stone around his heart.

Having drunk her fill of the view of the ocean,

Victoria turned, at the same time taking a step forward to begin her walk down the beach. So lulled by the peacefulness of the view, she'd forgotten how close her stoic companion was standing and bumped into him.

Lance's hands closed around her upper arms, steadying her. Her palms came to rest on his chest for added support and he felt deliciously solid, his grip sending rivers of fire coursing through her.

Lance ordered himself to release her, but his muscles refused to respond. Never had any woman felt so good to his touch. When she lifted her face to look up at him, his gaze riveted on her lips and for the second time he thought how kissable they looked...so soft, so full, so inviting. He told himself these were forbidden thoughts, but they remained, taunting him. Against his will his mouth moved toward hers.

Victoria's breath locked in her lungs. The enigmatic Captain Grayson was going to kiss her. A thrill of excitement flowed through her. His breath was warm and enticing against her skin, and even before his mouth found hers, her blood began to race and her heart pounded faster.

As if suddenly jerked awake, the captain abruptly straightened to a military stance and released her.

"Lance?" she said softly with gentle invitation, her voice letting him know she would not be displeased if he kissed her.

"It's lucky you did not twist your ankle," he said

coolly. "I would not have wanted to present you to your father in an injured condition."

Victoria regarded him in frustration. Not only was the cold Captain Grayson back, but he was subtly telling her that any intimacy between them would be considered by him to be an injury to her…a misuse of her that his duty would not permit. Clearly, there had been lust behind his desire to kiss her, but nothing more. Part of her knew she should be glad he was a man of honor and control. But another part still wanted that kiss. Anger toward herself for such weakness surged through her.

Determined to push the incident from her mind, she strode down the beach, trying to concentrate on the warm feel of the sand beneath her feet, every once in a while pausing to pick up a shell that interested her. But always she was aware of the man at her side. Constantly, she reminded herself that he'd made it clear he considered their relationship strictly business and did not even want to be her friend. Still, her curiosity about him continued to grow. "I suppose your parents are proud of you, you being the Head of the Investigative Division for the Grand Duke and all."

"I have no parents. I was raised in an orphanage." The words were out before Lance realized he'd spoken. Inwardly, he berated himself for responding. Talking about himself was one thing he never did.

Victoria paused to look at him. "I'm sorry."

"So were the nuns who got stuck with me."

"I would have thought you were an ideal child, always proper, always well-behaved."

Lance had never encountered so persistent a person as Victoria Rockford. Normally it took only one warning to keep people from prying into his private life. "The only thing you need to know about me is that I'm one of the best at what I do."

Victoria jerked as if he'd slapped her in the face for being too fresh. Pulling her gaze away from him, she continued down the beach.

He knew she was angry with him. He preferred it that way. If she was angry, maybe she wouldn't ask any more personal questions.

During the majority of the day Victoria managed not to exchange more than a few cursory words with Captain Grayson, but as they sat down to eat dinner, she broke her silence. He'd been on the phone with his men for nearly two hours discussing Malcolm's behavior and listening to the tape of Malcolm's interview and she wanted to know what was said.

"So what did your men learn when they interviewed Malcolm?"

"Not much."

When he said no more, Victoria glared at him. She'd learned her lesson. She would respect his desire to keep his private life private, but this concerned her and she would not settle for "not much."

"What *exactly* did he say when your men picked him up?"

Lance sighed. "He expressed shock that you had been kidnapped. He again declared that he'd been certain you were simply prolonging your vacation, particularly since he claims you called to tell him as much. Then he expressed relief that you were safe and asked when he might see you. That was what we expected his initial reaction to be."

"That's what I would have expected, as well." Victoria still did not want to believe Malcolm had been involved in her kidnapping. For twenty-seven years she'd thought of him as her father—not a good father, but her father nonetheless. "What did he say when he was told that I was the Grand Duke's daughter and not his?"

"He wasn't told. We wanted to give him the opportunity to slip up and tell us."

"And did he?" *Dumb question.* Malcolm was much too smart to make a slip like that.

"No."

"How did your fellow agents explain the fact that the Grand Duke's men were looking for me? I know Malcolm. He's a stickler for detail. He would have asked."

"He didn't. When my men showed up at his door, he acted as if he assumed it was your sister and Prince Damon who had brought us in on the case and asked us to find you. He made no reference to the Grand Duke being involved. When asked if he knew of any reason for you to be kidnapped, he said he didn't. He pointed out that he was not a wealthy man and that he had not been contacted for a ransom. He said he could only assume it was a madman with some perverted motive. He showed some alarm at this thought and asked if you had been harmed.''

"He actually showed alarm?" It wasn't like Malcolm to be emotional. Maybe Captain Grayson was wrong. Maybe Malcolm hadn't been involved.

"Yes," Lance answered.

She studied him narrowly. "But you don't believe it was genuine?"

"He is the most logical suspect. He knew about the birthmark and was privy to your travel plans. Then there was the cabin in which you were found."

Victoria knew that Malcolm could be a very good actor when it was required. She'd seen him saying the most horrible things behind someone's back and then being absolutely gracious to the same person to their face. "Did your men ask him about the cabin?"

"He said that whoever kidnapped you must have done a thorough job investigating you and him. He gave the same response when asked how the kidnapper would have known your travel plans."

For a long moment Victoria was silent, then she said, "He was a rotten father in most ways, but he did provide a roof over my head, food for me to eat and clothes to wear. He's also a proud man. If he has known all along that I wasn't his daughter, for him, he actually treated me fairly well. Perhaps he is innocent.''

"By your own admission, he's one of less than a handful of people who know about your birthmark. And, he has two strong motives. One is the money he hoped to collect, and the other is revenge...the woman he loved bore a child by another man. This was his chance to make the Grand Duke squirm.''

"I have never known Malcolm to forgive a slight and not pay back that slight when the opportunity arose,'' Victoria conceded. Her gaze dropped to her plate and she pushed the food around absently. ''I always wondered why my mother married him. I could tell she was afraid of him, and he was not always kind to her. He treated her like a possession. And there were many times he made her cry. Once when I was in my teens, I found her weeping and asked her why she didn't just leave him. She told me that his behavior was not entirely his fault, that she had to accept some of the blame. She refused to tell me why she felt that way. Now I understand.''

"Malcolm Rockford is a danger to you. Of that, I am certain,'' Lance said sternly. ''You must never forget that.'' He read the uncertainty on her face and knew from experience that no matter how badly a child was treated by a parent, they still wanted to believe that parent cared for him or her. ''You have to keep in mind that Rockford isn't your real father. And you must consider the timing. Your mother is dead. You said he treated her like a possession. It's possible he used you and the knowledge of your real father to keep her bound to him…a sort of blackmail. With her gone, he could seek his revenge.''

Victoria continued to stare at her food. What he said fit Malcolm's character like a glove. ''If that is what happened, I feel so sorry for my mother. She made one mistake and paid for it for the rest of her life.'' Her jaw tensed. ''That's not entirely true. Actually she made two mistakes. She loved the wrong man, then compounded her error by marrying an equally unsuitable man to hide her indiscretion from the world.''

''A perfect example of why people should not allow themselves to fall victim to love,'' Lance noted.

Victoria jerked her gaze to him. He had a point. Both her mother and sister had been victims of misplaced love. ''You're right.'' A bitter smile tilted one corner of her mouth. ''If I remain in your company long enough, perhaps I will become as cynical as you.''

Lance should have felt triumphant, but the thought of her becoming as jaded as he was bothered him. *At least she will be protected from the pain those who believe in love suffer,* he told himself.

Victoria's jaw firmed with resolve. ''I've changed my mind. I refuse to give up on love.''

''Then I wish you the best of luck because you will need it,'' he replied.

''I do not intend to rely on luck. I intend to rely

on good common sense and prudent judgment. When I fall in love, it will not be on a whim, and I won't be fooled by lust disguised as love. It will be the true, abiding type of love that is so deeply rooted not even the most devastating blows life can deliver will kill it.''

Lance read the purpose in her eyes. He had never known so determined a woman. For one brief instant he found himself wishing he was the one she was looking for. Immediately he shoved this thought from his mind. That was a path he forbade himself to follow. ''If anyone can succeed in such a quest, I am sure it will be you.''

Victoria looked stunned. ''I can't believe you didn't tell me I sounded like a fool.''

''I am aware that there are couples in this world who love each other the way you described.''

Victoria studied him narrowly. ''If you believe it exists, then why are you so adamant about not finding it for yourself.''

''I am not a loveable man. I accepted that fact long ago.''

''Maybe if you'd loosen up a little,'' Victoria suggested.

His jaw hardened. ''I am satisfied with who I am. I have no intention of changing.'' Lance stopped himself from further revelation. He'd spoken more openly to her than anyone he'd ever spoken to. She had a way of chipping away at the barrier he kept around his inner self, and he didn't like it. The sooner she was safely ensconced in the castle, the better.

Victoria suddenly found herself recalling the warm depths of Captain Grayson's eyes and the way his touch had spread a heat through her when he'd knelt before her. The man she'd seen in those few moments could win a woman's heart. Of course, she could not even be certain he really existed. She'd had no other glimpses of him. If he truly existed, the captain kept him locked deep inside. "I don't know about the unloveable part, but you are certainly a difficult man to get to know," she conceded.

Victoria frowned as a silence descended between them. Then she turned the frown on herself. She had other matters that should be occupying her mind. Her whole life was changing, and she was not convinced it was going to be for the better. In the past she'd had only Malcolm's disdain to deal with. Captain Grayson had assured her that she would be welcomed by the Grand Duke, his wife and sons, but she wasn't convinced of that. Again her gaze shifted to her host. "This wall you are determined to keep between me and you...is it a normal thing with you? I mean, do you keep everyone at a distance?"

He said coldly, "By remaining detached, I can perform my duties much more efficiently."

Victoria regarded him with cool command. "I wasn't trying to get personal, I was just wondering if I could learn to be the way you are. Then I wouldn't have to be anxious about my reception at the castle. I wouldn't care.''

''You have no need to worry about your reception at the castle,'' he assured her.

''That's easy for you to say,'' Victoria returned skeptically. ''You're so determined to keep yourself emotionally closed off, I wouldn't be surprised to discover you've been blind to all sorts of bubbling hostilities inside the castle walls.''

''I am very aware of the emotions of others. That's an essential part of my job.''

Victoria remained unconvinced, but decided that pursuing the subject would be futile. She started to turn her full attention to her dinner, then recalled their conversation earlier in the day. ''Did you find out anything about Crenshaw?''

''According to new information, he and Malcolm had a falling-out a while back and have been rather cool toward each other since.''

''Why am I not surprised?'' Victoria muttered dryly. ''Eventually Malcolm has a falling-out with everyone.'' Tired of thinking about Malcolm and how her world had forever changed, Victoria concentrated on her meal.

Chapter Five

The next morning, following breakfast, Victoria sat on the porch sipping her second cup of coffee. Captain Grayson was inside on the phone.

"I'm not certain that's such a good idea," she heard him saying. After a few more minutes, she heard his grim acquiescence. "Yes, sir. If that is the Grand Duke's command, it will be obeyed."

Her body tensed. *What now?*

Stepping out onto the porch, Lance remained standing while he addressed her. "The Grand Duke wishes to meet you."

"But you don't think that's such a good idea." She repeated what she'd heard him say. Her eyes challenged him. "Is that because you lied when you said I would be welcomed?"

"It's because I'm concerned about your safety.

However, there is a secret passage into the castle. We'll go in under cover of darkness. I should be able to get you in and out without any outsider—or even very many of the insiders—being the wiser." Having made this pronouncement, he went back inside to call in all the arrangements.

Left alone on the porch, Victoria could feel her nervousness growing by leaps and bounds. Although she'd known that eventually she would meet the Grand Duke, she realized now that she wasn't prepared. Meeting her real father for the first time was certain to be a difficult moment. His being the Grand Duke made it even more so. Pride demanded that she make a good impression or, at least, present herself with dignity. Leaving the porch, she went to Captain Grayson, who was still on the phone in the living room issuing orders to his men, while keeping an eye on her. What amazed her was that she found his constant watchfulness comforting. Normally, to have someone following her every movement would have been an annoyance.

I am still shaken by my kidnapping, she reasoned. It was only natural that she would feel safer knowing someone was always watching over her.

"Jason's wife is due to have her baby in the next few days, isn't she?" Lance asked curtly.

Victoria decided the answer must have been in the affirmative because next he said, "I thought so. Send him home. Bring in Ryan to take his place."

After a few more orders were issued, he hung up

and she grinned at him. "You're not as tough as you want people to think."

His expression frosty, he raised a questioning eyebrow.

"I heard you just now. You let one of your men go home because his wife is having a baby. The Captain Grayson I thought I knew would have made the man stay in the field and fulfill his *duty.*"

Lance gave her an impatient look. "I sent him home because I knew that no matter how hard he tried to keep his mind on his job, it would only be half there and that's not good enough. Your life could be in danger and it's my job to see that you're protected as completely as is humanly possible."

She continued to regard him thoughtfully. "You really hate admitting that you have a softer side, don't you?"

He scowled. So maybe he had wanted Jason to be able to be at his wife's side when their child was born. It was his way of wishing the child well. But he was not willing to admit that to Victoria Rockford. She had already seen chinks in his armor that no one else had been privy to. She would see no more. "I am merely being practical. You will be disappointed if you read more than that into my actions."

Victoria frowned back at him. "Well, whatever your reasons, what you did was very nice."

Lance regarded her coolly. "Did you come looking for me for a reason?"

"As a matter of fact, I did. I need to know how to behave when I meet the Grand Duke."

Her statement surprised him. "I would suggest you behave with decorum," he replied dryly.

Victoria grinned. "Not only do you have a secret streak of kindness, you have a sense of humor."

Most people never realized when he was jesting. That she could so easily read him made him uneasy. "What exactly do you want to know about your meeting with the Grand Duke?" he asked, his manner starkly businesslike.

"So you don't want to admit to a sense of humor, either? I have never met a man so intent on keeping his humanity hidden. Is it some sort of macho thing with you?"

Again Lance allowed his impatience to show. "You are persistent. If I don't fault you for prying and you don't fault me for wanting to keep my private thoughts private, then we can call ourselves even and get on with whatever it is you want to know about meeting the Grand Duke."

For a long moment Victoria regarded him in silence. This really wasn't like her. Normally she respected other people's desire not to have their lives pried into. *It's ridiculous, foolish, very close to schoolgirlish, to be so curious about a man who is so determined to keep me at a distance,* she admonished herself. "As you wish," she conceded, vowing not to pry again. Then, turning her mind to the coming meeting, she said, "How do I address the

Grand Duke? Do I curtsy? Should I wear a suit or a dress?''

''I would suggest you address him as 'Your Royal Highness' to begin with. It's my guess that he will tell you what to call him after that. And you should not speak until he has spoken to you.''

So don't start babbling from nervousness, she ordered herself. Aloud, she said, ''Okay, I've got that.''

''I would also suggest that you do curtsy. But don't try to curtsy too deeply. I've seen too many women falter. It makes them look clumsy. Make it a medium curtsy.''

Performing a medium curtsy, Victoria experienced a rush of anxiety as her body swayed slightly. ''I guess I'd better practice that today.''

Even clumsy, she was beautiful, Lance thought. He could not imagine the Grand Duke being anything but pleased with her. ''I'm sure you'll do just fine.''

''Will you be there?''

''I'll be right outside the Grand Duke's chambers.'' Lance wished he could remain at her side to see her through this first meeting with her father. In the next instant, he was berating himself for being so concerned about so personal a matter. Her physical well-being should be his only concern.

Victoria couldn't believe she'd practically asked him to remain by her side. That she had come to rely on his presence so greatly bothered her. Until he'd entered her life, she'd grown used to standing on her own two feet. And it was clear he didn't want to be her champion. Besides, she didn't need one. "Yes, of course," she replied, stiffly.

Returning the conversation to her original questions, he said, "As for clothing, I would say that either a suit or a dress would suffice."

Victoria thanked him for his advice, then went to her room and began pulling clothes out of her suitcases. It took a while but she finally chose her gray pin-stripe suit. She'd packed a pink blouse to wear with it for a coquettish touch of color. Now she wished she had her simple white one. Even worse, the only heels she had to go with the outfit were a new pair of white sling-back stilettos she'd bought just for her vacation. They'd made her feel sexy. Right at this moment she would have paid double for a pair of the sensible, low-heeled shoes she wore to work. "But they do look great," she murmured, determined to find a bright side. "And with practice, I should be able to curtsy in them without breaking my neck."

A few hours later, Victoria nervously made one final inspection of herself in the mirror then went in search of Captain Grayson. As she entered the living room, he rose abruptly as if he suddenly considered it a dereliction of duty to have been discovered seated.

"Your Highness," he said stiffly, performing a very low bow.

"I hope that means I look all right for my audience with the Grand Duke," she quipped to cover her surprise at his intense level of formality.

"You look very nice," he replied, straightening to the military posture she'd grown used to seeing. "We should be on our way."

She knew her nervousness about meeting with the Grand Duke was making her hypersensitive. Still, Captain Grayson's new level of deference startled her. A fresh bout of anxiety swept through her. Remaining where she was, she studied him narrowly. "Was there a change in my status while I was in the bedroom that I should know about?"

He said coolly, "I thought I would prepare you for how you will be treated when you enter the castle. Of course, some may not bow so low and others will salute. But I thought it would be wise to demonstrate the ultimate of respect. Now you will not show surprise at what awaits you."

Victoria grudgingly admitted that she'd been hoping for a compliment…that he'd say she was so stunning, he couldn't resist bowing to her. In the next instant she was mocking herself. Captain Grayson was not a man who easily gave in to emotions. "I am grateful," she said honestly. "And how am I expected to respond?"

"With a slight nod of your head. Like so." He demonstrated.

Victoria mimicked him, then drew a shaky sigh. "All right. Now I'm ready."

In spite of her declaration, Lance saw the continued anxiousness in her features. "You'll do just fine. I'm certain when the Grand Duke sees you, he will be greatly pleased."

Victoria looked hard into his face. "Do you really mean that?"

He met her gaze levelly. "Yes."

"Thank you."

Lance saw her anxiety decrease. Before he realized what was happening, one corner of his mouth tilted upward into a crooked smile.

Victoria smiled back. "I'll bet those muscles were surprised. It's a wonder they actually worked."

Lance had to struggle to keep his indifferent demeanor in place. She made him actually want to laugh. Perhaps as little as a week from now she would be ensconced within the royal family and barely notice his presence, he reminded himself curtly, repairing the newest dent she'd made in his armor.

Victoria shook her head. "I am beginning to believe that you really are proof that what our mothers always warn us about is true. A face can become frozen in a single expression."

Lance opened the door. "We really should be on our way."

Not wanting to be late for her first meeting with

her real father, Victoria nodded and preceded him out of the house.

"Why didn't you warn me that I should bring along my sneakers to wear until we reached the castle," she grumbled at Lance Grayson's back as she followed him through the stone-walled tunnel that led to the secret entrance. The floor was hardened dirt and spiderwebs along the sides gave evidence that the passage had not been used in some time.

"Warts on rats!" she cursed, stumbling on the uneven ground and nearly falling. Coming to a halt to fully regain her balance, she glared at her feet. They hurt. "These heels are made for dancing, not hiking."

Lance stopped and turned back. Reaching her in one long stride, he scooped her up into his arms.

Victoria's protest died in her throat as rivers of fire coursed through her. She did not understand how a man who was so determined to keep himself at a distance from others could ignite her body by his mere touch. Wrapping her arms around his neck for better support, she studied his taut profile. He didn't look the least bit pleased. Anger at herself for being attracted to a man who obviously considered her a nuisance cooled the fires raging through her. "Put me down."

Lance had been trying very hard to think of her as something along the lines of a sack of potatoes. It hadn't worked. She was much too soft and her curves taunted him with erotic sensations. Given a choice, he would have gladly obeyed. But he had no choice. He could not allow her to injure herself. "It is my duty to bring you safely to your father."

"I insist you set me down," she demanded, attempting to wiggle free.

The movement of her body against his was more than Lance could fight. He felt his arousal becoming evident. "Behave!" he growled.

Victoria froze. It took some very stern mental and physical effort, but Lance managed to get his body under control by the time they reached the entrance to the castle.

Pressed against his chest, Victoria felt his heart pounding strong and rapid. Her gaze went to his neck and she discovered she could actually see his pulse throbbing. That could be due to the exertion of carrying her, she conceded. Or, it could be something else. A smile played at the corners of her mouth. She liked the idea of it being "something else." In fact, she liked that idea very much.

With a sigh, Lance stood her on the floor before a heavy tapestry. She let her hands run slowly from his shoulders down over his chest as she took her time to steady herself. Her gaze never leaving his face, she said with a flirtatious edge, "Thanks for the lift."

Lance concentrated on a spot beyond her shoulders. "You're welcome."

Acutely aware of his attempt to avoid eye contact,

Victoria grinned to herself as her suspicion that Captain Grayson wasn't as immune to her as he wanted her to believe grew.

Stepping away from her, he pulled aside the tapestry that hid a door.

Victoria passed him and found herself in a small, elegantly furnished anteroom.

Taking the lead, Lance guided her through a maze of corridors and up a flight of stairs to a pair of floor-to-ceiling wooden doors. A forest scene with wild animals had been carved into the doors. Sentries stood on either side of them. The sentries stiffened to full attention at her approach.

Reaching the door, Lance knocked. Almost immediately it was opened from the inside and he stepped aside, taking his position outside the room.

Victoria's heart pounded with trepidation. Her gaze riveted on Captain Grayson and she found herself wishing with all her heart that he was accompanying her. His mere presence gave her strength. In the next instant she was berating herself for being so cowardly. Her head held high with dignity, she entered the Grand Duke's chambers.

Victor Thorton rose to greet her. "At last we meet," he said, striding toward her.

He looked even more impressive in person than he did in newspaper photographs, Victoria thought. Tall, with silver-gray hair and blue eyes, he had a regal bearing.

With a wave of his hand Victor dismissed the

others in the room. Remembering her manners, Victoria curtsied as he neared her. When she lifted her head, she discovered they were alone.

"You are definitely a Thorton," Victor said with approval. "And most certainly one of the loveliest. You rival your great-aunt Helen's beauty and she was considered one of the most beautiful women of her day."

Victoria blushed with pleasure. Her father was definitely a charmer. "You're very kind."

"Come sit with me." The Grand Duke motioned her toward a pair of chairs in front of the fireplace.

Her nerves remaining taut, Victoria preceded him to the chairs. She was seating herself when it occurred to her that she probably wasn't supposed to sit down before he did. Immediately she straightened, then felt like a jack-in-the-box and wondered if she'd looked as ridiculous. "This is awkward," she confessed. "I'm not certain what the protocol is."

The Grand Duke smiled. "Good. You must always speak your mind to me when we're alone. And you're right. This is awkward. But you'll learn protocol with time. For now, you must behave as if we are nothing more than a father and daughter." He motioned toward her chair. "Please, sit."

Victoria obeyed. "None of this seems real."

Victor moved his chair closer to hers, then seated himself. "I can see your mother in your eyes." His manner became solemn. "I will not lie to you and say that I loved her. But I was wildly infatuated with her. When she smiled, it was as if a second sun had suddenly appeared to warm and brighten the day. And when she laughed, it was like bells ringing. She was so carefree, so full of life, so joyful.''

Victoria had never thought of her mother in those terms. The Maribelle Rockford she'd known had been subdued and rarely laughed. ''She changed,'' she said simply.

Apology etched itself in the Grand Duke's features. ''She knew I had a wife and son and that duty would not allow me to abandon them.'' He leaned closer and took Victoria's hands in his. ''But I swear to you, if I had known Maribelle was carrying my child, I would have helped her and you. I would not have abandoned my wife and son, but I would not have abandoned you and your mother, either.''

Victoria guessed the ''help'' he would have provided would have been to hide them away, most likely in another country. However, she would not fault him. When he had learned of her existence, he had not tried to deny her. ''What is past, is past. It cannot be changed. I am grateful that you acknowledged me and sent Captain Grayson to find me. I know this cannot be easy for you or the Duchess.'' Thought of the Duchess brought a fresh wave of anxiety. Was the woman truly ready to accept her? ''Especially for the Duchess,'' she added, letting her worry show openly.

Victor smiled encouragingly. ''My marriage to

Sara was an arranged one. We wed out of duty to our families. But through the years we have learned to love each other and, more importantly, we have become friends. She has forgiven me my transgression."

She might have forgiven her husband, but was she really ready to accept his illegitimate daughter? Victoria wondered. Memories of her life with Malcolm came rushing back. "My youth was unpleasant. Now I realize that was most likely because the man I thought was my father was not and knew he was not and resented me. I do not want to step back into that same kind of situation. I would prefer to continue living on my own."

"That is no longer possible. Too many people now know of your existence. It would not be safe for you to go into the world unprotected. But even more importantly, I am determined to right the wrong I have done you and get to know you as a father should know a daughter." Taking her hands in his, he gave them a squeeze. "Life here will not be as it was with Malcolm Rockford. Sara is a kindhearted, gracious woman who understands that you had no control over the circumstances of your birth."

Silently, Victoria promised herself that if his words did not prove true, she would strike out on her own, with or without his blessing. "I hope you're reading her correctly. I don't wish to bring either of you any unhappiness."

"I'm the one who has caused what strain there is between my wife and myself." From a nearby table, he produced a paper. "I would very much like for you to sign this now so that you will be my daughter legally from this moment on."

Victoria stared at the legal document. Captain Grayson had told her the Grand Duke had had the papers drawn up to adopt her, but she was still having trouble adjusting to the reality of the situation.

Victor handed her a pen. "Just place your signature on that line," he instructed.

Still uncertain of what the future held, she did like the idea of ridding herself of Malcolm's name and signed.

Victor returned the paper to the table, then gave her hands another squeeze and smiled warmly. "I've been informed that Captain Grayson is still uncertain as to who else may be involved in your kidnapping and as such wishes to keep you hidden. I don't want to believe that anyone in the castle could be involved, but I'm not willing to risk your life. So I'll keep this meeting short as promised. When I'm assured you're safe, we'll have a long visit and you'll tell me all about yourself."

Realizing their meeting had come to an end, Victoria rose with her father. Inwardly, she breathed a sigh of relief. Although the Grand Duke had been very nice, she had not been able to relax in his presence. He was still a stranger and she needed time to get used to her new situation.

"I must also apologize for the need to keep you hidden away. But Captain Grayson is the very best at what he does. I would not feel safe trusting your life to anyone else."

"He has been most gracious to me."

The Grand Duke raised an eyebrow. "I've heard him described as dutiful, correct in his manner and coldly efficient, but I have never, nor did I ever expect to hear the word *gracious* used in reference to him."

"He is all you have said," she admitted. "But I owe him my life and that has made me rather fond of him in spite of his coolness."

The Grand Duke grinned. "From all I've heard regarding our captain, he is not used to having people feel fondly toward him. He seems, actually, to discourage it. How is he reacting to your friendliness?"

Victoria breathed a frustrated sigh. "He refuses to allow it."

Victor's expression became fatherly. "He grew up tough in one of the less desirable parts of Thortonburg. He's the kind of man you want by your side in times of trouble, but he's a man who still carries many secrets locked inside."

"I will keep what you have said in mind."

"And I'll pray that we can move you into the castle very soon." He gave her a hug, then opened the door for her himself.

Victoria curtsied, then exited. Once in the corridor, she looked for Captain Grayson. Spotting him standing to one side, she felt herself relaxing and realized he was like an anchor in this storm of newness and uncertainty into which she had been swept. Wondering how he would feel if she confessed that to him, she walked toward him.

"Did your meeting go well?"

Victoria could barely believe her ears. Captain Grayson was prying into her personal life about a matter that did not involve her kidnapping. That was a barrier he had, until this moment, been determined not to cross. Pleased by this show of interest in her welfare, she smiled. "Yes. As you assured me, he was very kind."

His stance suddenly became more rigid. "We should be leaving."

Clearly he was not happy with himself for letting down his guard for even one moment and acting like a friend, Victoria noted. Again she wondered what made him so determined to remain apart from others.

Taking the lead, Lance started down the corridor. They had gone only a few paces when a woman stepped out from a side corridor and came toward them. Realizing she was not going to step aside and let them pass, Lance stopped, shielding Victoria with his body.

The woman gave Lance a wary glance. Peering around him at Victoria, she curtsied and said with deference, "The Duchess requests an audience."

Lance scowled. "No one but the Grand Duke was to even have known she was coming."

Fear showed on the woman's face and her shoulders squared as if to say she was doing her duty and no one was going to stop her. "The Grand Duke and the Duchess aren't keeping any more secrets from each other."

"I don't like this," Lance growled.

Victoria wasn't looking forward to facing the Duchess. In the woman's eyes, she had to be a symbol of betrayal. However, this meeting had to take place sooner or later. "I cannot refuse."

Lance tried to tell himself that it was only her physical safety that guided him, but he knew that was a lie. Although he had never seen or heard of the Duchess behaving meanly toward anyone, he worried that she might be harboring a deep resentment toward Victoria. *It's not my duty to protect the princess from the Duchess,* he told himself. Still, the urge remained. "There are too many places within these walls where a person can hide and attack by surprise."

The servant regarded him indignantly. "You can't possibly believe that someone here is involved."

"Until I apprehend the culprits, I cannot be certain who is and who is not involved."

The woman issued a snort and turned her attention back to Victoria. "Will you accompany me, Your Highness?"

Victoria didn't think she really had a choice. Refusing could cause the Duchess to feel slighted. "Yes."

"All right. Let's get this over with." Lance took a rear position, letting the maid lead the way.

Remember to curtsy and don't fall on your face, Victoria repeated to herself over and over again, trying to quell a rush of panic. *If she doesn't like me, I simply won't come back,* she told herself as her nervousness increased to the point of nausea.

When they reached the Duchess's chambers, the maid opened the door, then stepped aside to allow Victoria to enter. Lance followed her inside and waited silently while Victoria curtsied.

Sara Thorton, Grand Duchess of Thortonburg, a petite, handsome woman with delicate features, looked mildly disconcerted by his presence. "I wanted a few words in private with Victoria."

Lance bowed low. "I merely entered to request that, for her safety, you keep this meeting short."

Sara frowned. "Surely you cannot believe she is in danger here."

"It is my belief that Malcolm Rockford is primarily responsible for her kidnapping. However, his accomplice could be someone close to you and the Grand Duke."

The Duchess sighed. "As usual, you're right to be cautious. I'll be brief."

"Thank you, Your Highness." Lance bowed low to show deference.

As he exited, the Duchess dismissed the woman

who had led them there and another maid who was
in the room. Waiting until the door was closed, she
then motioned toward some chairs grouped by the
fireplace. "Please be seated."

There was a cool guardedness in the Duchess's
manner that strained Victoria's nerves even more.
She started toward the chairs, but in mid-stride her
nerves snapped. Turning back to the Duchess, she
said, "I realize I must be an embarrassment to you
and I do apologize."

Some of the stiffness in the Duchess's manner
softened. "You're not to blame for anything that has
happened."

Victoria had lived too much of her life behind a
curtain of prudent silence. She would not go back
to living that way. Whatever the Duchess felt toward
her, she wanted it out in the open. "That does not
make this any less uncomfortable for you or me."

The Duchess nodded with approval. "I like your
bluntness. And you're right, this is an uncomfortable
situation. However, I have forgiven my husband.
And I will not hold his indiscretion against you."

Victoria could not help but admire the woman's
strength. "You are most gracious."

The Duchess walked to a table and picked up an
album. "I have prepared this for you. It contains
photos of family members as well as staff. All are
labeled. I thought it might be a help to you to become acquainted with them by sight. That way you

won't have so many new names and faces to put together when you move into the castle.''

Clearly the Duchess was attempting to make her transition into the family as painless as possible. ''Thank you,'' Victoria said, accepting the album.

The Duchess met her gaze levelly. ''It is my sincerest wish that we will become friends. I've always wanted a daughter.''

Victoria read the honesty in the woman's eyes. ''I would like that very much.''

Sara drew a deep breath, then released it and smiled. ''I would say our first meeting has gone well.''

Realizing the Duchess had been as nervous as she had been, Victoria smiled back. ''Very well,'' she agreed.

Sara's gaze turned to the door. ''I'm sure Captain Grayson is growing impatient.'' In the next breath, she added, ''Although a person would be hard-pressed to know anything about what he is thinking and feeling for certain.''

''He can be rather enigmatic,'' Victoria conceded.

Sara turned to her. ''I confess he intimidates me. But he's the best at what he does.''

''I find his company reassuring.''

Sara nodded. ''Yes, under the circumstances, I would, too. However, hopefully your kidnappers will be apprehended soon and you'll be free to go about as you please.''

Victoria forced a smile, but the thought of losing Captain Grayson's company didn't make her happy.

A short while later, as she followed the captain to the secret passage, it occurred to her that these feelings she was experiencing toward him could be merely gratitude for saving her. He had done nothing to encourage her to feel friendly toward him. It didn't seem logical that she should honestly be attracted to him.

Still, she found herself looking forward to being carried down the secret passage. But as they entered the dirt-floored tunnel, he nodded toward a pair of sneakers.

"I had one of my people find those for you," he said. "They may not be a perfect fit, but they should suffice."

Obviously he didn't want to repeat their earlier trek. Fighting back a surge of disappointment, Victoria changed into the sneakers. She should remember that Captain Grayson refused even to consider being her friend. Still, as they continued down the corridor, she couldn't stop herself from wondering about her silent companion and wanting to know what had happened to make him so determined to keep the rest of the world at arm's length.

Chapter Six

Victoria awoke the next morning feeling restless. Going into the kitchen, she poured herself a cup of coffee then went out onto the porch. Captain Grayson was there, his usual shuttered expression in place. He'd been sitting in a relaxed posture with his feet propped on the rail. At her approach, he rose and came to attention.

"You really don't have to do that every time I join you," she said.

"You're a princess. It is only proper to show deference," he replied, waiting until she seated herself before again seating himself.

Taking a sip of her coffee, Victoria stared out at the ocean. "My whole world has been turned topsy-turvy." She said aloud what had been on her mind.

Her gaze swung to her stoic companion. "I need someone to talk to and you get elected."

He remained silent.

She was not surprised when he said nothing. She hadn't expected him to. In fact, she was willing to wager that this would be a totally one-sided conversation, but she didn't care. There were feelings she needed to work out, and talking about them seemed to be the only way. "A part of me says I should be happy, even joyful. I now have a reason why Malcolm treated me as he did. To be honest, down deep inside I've always worried that there was some defect in me."

Pausing, she frowned at him. "At this point you're supposed to tell me that I'm a very nice person and not the least bit defective. Or maybe just a little, but no more than any normal person." Wondering if he really would say something, she wagered that he wouldn't.

"You're one of the least defective people I've met."

Surprised, she studied him speculatively. "That sounded very close to a compliment."

"I was merely stating a fact."

That he thought well of her made her feel like a child at Christmas who had just gotten the one present she most wanted.

"Well, I'm going to take it as a compliment anyway."

"You may take it anyway you wish."

"Thank you," she replied, experiencing some frustration at his continued detachment. Then telling herself that he was the way he was and she must accept him as such, she turned her mind back to the concerns that had prompted her to seek out someone to talk to. "I tell myself that I should be excited about being a princess...a real-life princess. Then I immediately ask myself why. It's not like I'm some-one the royal family is all that thrilled to have dis-covered existed. I'm the Grand Duke's illegitimate daughter...more a source of embarrassment than pride."

"Is that how the Duchess treated you? As a source of embarrassment?"

Victoria was certain she heard a protective edge in his voice. "No, she was very kind, just as you described her." Her gaze narrowed on him. "I could swear you actually sounded like a concerned friend."

He said stiffly, "I'm merely concerned with fair-ness. It isn't right for anyone to condemn you for the circumstances of your birth."

Victoria recalled what the Grand Duke said about Captain Grayson's early years. "Are you speaking from experience? Have people unjustly condemned you for the circumstances of your birth?"

"No."

The firmness in his tone warned Victoria that she was treading on unsafe ground, but this time her curiosity would not be quelled. She was not certain why, but she needed to know what made this man tick. Even more, she wanted to heal the wounds that had made him so insular. "I don't believe you. I think that's why you refuse to let anyone be a friend. You're afraid they'll find out about your past and then won't like you anymore. Well, I can assure you that I'm not that shallow."

He gave her a dry look. "At the age of twelve, I ran away from the orphanage and took up life on the streets. Before I could even walk, my father had taught me to pick locks. He'd been a thief and, like father, like son, I made my living by stealing. Once, I even stole a wallet from a dead man who'd been hit by a car."

Victoria realized he was trying to shock her into disliking him. But all she could picture was a lonely little boy trying to survive. "You have clearly redeemed yourself. A true friend would not hold your past against you."

He stared out at the ocean. The grim set of his jaw coupled with his silence told her that he considered their conversation over. But she couldn't stop wondering about the young, ragged, dark-haired boy trying to survive on his own. "So why did you run away from the orphanage?"

Lance turned to glower at her. "I got tired of being there."

Victoria glowered back. "You don't just give up food and shelter because you're tired of it."

"And you don't know when to stop, do you?" he growled back.

A part of her wanted to, but from somewhere deep inside an even stronger part refused. "You saved my life. I figure I owe you for that and I intend to repay it by being your friend."

"I do not need your friendship. I'm perfectly content with my life just the way it is."

She could almost see the door he was intent on closing between them. "Well, everyone needs a friend and I'm going to be yours whether you like it or not."

"I do not *need* anyone," he snarled.

The urge to scream in frustration was almost overwhelming. Again she wondered why it felt so necessary to befriend this man. *Payback for saving my life,* she told herself. Aloud she demanded impatiently, "Why are you so afraid to let anyone get close to you?"

"It isn't fear. I simply don't like being disappointed."

"I'm not a fair-weather kind of friend. When I make someone my friend, I stick by that friendship through thick and thin."

Anger toward a hurt buried deep within surfaced to etch itself into his features. "Even my own mother didn't want me. My father died when I was five. When I was six, she announced she'd had her fill of raising me on her own and left me at the orphanage. I can still remember begging her to keep me. But she never even looked back.''

In her mind's eye, Victoria saw him as a small child, frightened and feeling deserted. With every fiber of her being, she wanted to help him get over that pain. ''She could have just been going through a difficult time. She could have been suffering from depression.''

He glowered at her attempt to find a good reason for his abandonment. ''I ran away from the orphanage to find her. I thought that since I'd grown up enough to take care of myself, she'd take me back. It took a while. I was sixteen before I tracked her down. She'd remarried. She had a nice home, a husband who made good money and three children. She told me that she didn't want me back, that she'd never wanted me in the first place and that she wanted me out of her life. She said she'd only married my father because he'd gotten her pregnant. She said he'd been a deadbeat, that he hadn't even been a successful thief and she expected me to end up as badly as he had. Then she wrote me a check and told me to never darken her door again.''

Victoria had never felt such rage toward another person. She wished she could face this soulless woman and tell her what she thought of her. Aloud, she said, ''But you didn't turn out badly as she predicted.''

''No, I didn't.'' Pride showed in his features. ''I chose to prove her wrong. I got myself a job, went back to school and when I turned eighteen, I enlisted in the military. My street smarts proved to be a valuable asset and got me into the Intelligence Division.''

Determined to make him understand that he was robbing himself by refusing to let anyone get close, she said, ''Just like you didn't let her prediction about your future prove true, you shouldn't let your mother's desertion keep you from forming friendships.''

He regarded her dryly. ''I tried making friends in the orphanage. But my 'friends' would leave and never come back. Out on the street, I learned that those who wanted my friendship wanted something in return. So thanks, but no thanks.'' His stoic mask again in place, he rose. ''Like I said, I prefer my life just the way it is.''

Victoria watched in silence as he strode into the house. Captain Lance Grayson was definitely a hard man...very comparable to a stone mountain. She wished she could heal the wounds that made him the way he was, but she doubted she could ever break through the defenses he kept around himself. Still, she would be his friend, even if it was a one-sided friendship. She owed him that much.

Victoria sipped her coffee absently. She understood Captain Grayson's need to face his mother. She was feeling that same kind of need. Her jaw hardening into a firm line, she went in search of her host. She found him in the kitchen setting boxes of cereal on the table for her to choose from for her breakfast.

Early on she'd discovered that he didn't cook and didn't keep any food around other than cereal and frozen dinners. And since she hadn't been in the mood to cook, that had suited her just fine. Suddenly she had the most tremendous urge to prepare a real home-cooked meal for him, but not today. Today, she had something else that needed to be done. "Where is Malcolm? Do you still have him in custody?"

"No, he's home. He maintained his innocence throughout our interrogation and since we have no solid evidence against him we were forced to release him. But I have men watching him twenty-four hours a day."

"I want to go see him."

"That's not a good idea." His tone told her that he refused to allow this.

Her resolve deepened. "I have to face him. I have to know if he was really involved in my kidnapping."

"He'll just deny it."

"I think I'll know if he's lying." Her back straightened with determination. "I have to do this. And I will go, with or without you."

For a long moment, Lance regarded her in silence. He didn't doubt she meant what she said. Locking her up to prevent her from leaving was not an option. He knew her well enough to know she would fight him tooth and nail if he tried that. Besides, they needed a break in this case. Maybe her facing Malcolm would cause the man to slip up and provide proof of his guilt, perhaps even reveal his accomplice or accomplices. "All right, but we do this my way."

Victoria breathed a sigh of relief. "Whatever you say, you're the boss."

He gave her a wry look. "I'm the boss as long as you get your way."

"Works for me," she quipped. Ignoring the boxes of cereal, she popped open a box of breakfast bars, took one for herself and tossed one to him. "So, let's get going."

As they neared Thortonburg, Victoria's stomach tightened. "You haven't let anyone warn Malcolm that I'm coming, have you? I don't want him to have a chance to prepare."

"No. Even my own men don't know we're coming."

She raised an eyebrow questioningly.

"I decided that it would be safest if no one had advance notice of your visit."

Victoria was beginning to recognize more and more of his tiny nuances. The faintest hint of hesitation in his voice told her he was holding back on her. "You suspect that one of your own men could be involved?"

"No, not one of my men. I simply didn't want to

take any chances. Surprise and keeping the enemy off guard are always advantages.''

''Why do I get the feeling you're not telling me everything?''

''I don't like making unfounded accusations.''

Knowing from the set of his jaw he wasn't going to say any more, Victoria gave him an impatient glare, then sat back in her seat and considered what she would say to Malcolm.

When they reached the outskirts of Thortonburg, Lance said, ''Slide down in your seat so that no one can see you.''

As she obeyed, he pulled off onto a side road, then placed a call to his men. Following a quick conversation, he hung up. ''According to the two men I have watching Malcolm, he's home alone. We'll give the rest of my men a few minutes to surround the place, then I'll take you in.''

Victoria nodded her agreement and took several calming breaths in an attempt to steady her nerves. It didn't work. ''Even under the best of circumstances, I've always hated facing Malcolm,'' she confessed, too tense to remain silent. ''He used to insist that I ask his permission anytime I wanted to do anything with a friend or go on a date or attend a dance…just anything. My mother tried to tell me that this was because he was concerned about my welfare, but I was certain from a very early age that he was only doing it because he liked having control over my life. Even after I moved out from under his roof, he would still try to control me and when I rebelled he would threaten not to allow me to see my mother.'' Hot tears of anger welled in her eyes. ''When she was on her deathbed, he tried to keep me away from her and he refused to allow us any privacy to say our goodbyes. I don't know why I have any doubt as to the depth of his villainy.''

''So why face him? Let me call this off and get you out of here.''

Victoria blinked back the hot tears. ''No. If he was involved in my kidnapping, I want him to know that he can't intimidate me or cause me to cower.''

Lance continued to scan their surroundings, looking for any possible threat. ''You're letting pride rule reason.''

''Maybe. But it's something I have to do,'' she insisted.

He checked his watch. It was time. Starting the car, he drove to Malcolm's. ''I'm coming in with you,'' he said, his tone letting her know that this was not a point for discussion.

Victoria considered protesting. She didn't want Malcolm to think she was afraid to face him alone. However, if he was as black-hearted as it appeared he might be, she would be stupid not to accept protection. Besides, Captain Grayson's presence gave her courage and a feeling of security, and for this meeting she needed all the support she could muster. ''Fine,'' she replied. Then recalling what he'd told her about the interview his men had conducted with

Malcolm, she said, "You told me that your men did not inform Malcolm that he wasn't my real father."

"That's right," Lance confirmed. "No one, not even my contact with the Thortonburg police, has been informed of that."

At Malcolm's, Lance parked in front, then escorted her to the door.

She knocked. Ever since the first day she'd had her own place, she'd knocked when she returned here. Even though this had been her home for the majority of her life, she'd never felt comfortable simply walking in. From within, she heard footfalls and pictured Malcolm, tall, lean with harshly angular features, approaching. Knowing he had reached the door, she felt her back stiffen. It was a learned habit. From as early as age five she could recall physically bracing herself for any encounter with him.

"Victoria. How wonderful to see you looking so well," he greeted her.

For a moment, Victoria could only stare in stunned silence. He was smiling at her. It looked unnatural and strained as if his facial muscles were having trouble conforming to this friendly configuration. Steeling herself, she met his gaze. For as long as she could remember there had been only coldness in his eyes when he looked at her. Today they were shuttered. "May I come in?"

"Yes, of course. This is your home," he effused, stepping aside to allow her and Lance to enter.

He never tried to make me feel like this was my home before, Victoria thought cynically. Continuing into the living room, she remained standing. Lance took a position slightly behind her.

Malcolm followed, pausing as he reached Lance. "I'm Malcolm Rockford." He extended his hand.

"Captain Lance Grayson, Head of the Investigative Division of the Royal Security Detail." Accepting the handshake, Lance noticed a slight clenching of Malcolm's jaw...a sign the man was holding himself under tight control. Lance's instincts warned him that this man was dangerous.

"I am so very grateful to you for saving my daughter's life."

Lance noted that Malcolm's friendly demeanor was not reflected in his eyes. Instead, the man studied him guardedly.

Having acknowledged him, Malcolm turned his attention to Victoria. Approaching her in one long stride, he gave her a hug. "I'm so glad you're safe."

Every instinct Lance had rebelled at allowing the man to touch her. It took all of his control not to grab Malcolm and pull him away from her.

Victoria was frozen by amazement. Malcolm never hugged her. His touch felt unnatural and left her with a chill.

Stepping back, Malcolm continued with apology, "I should have listened to your sister's concerns more closely. But you've always been so strong-willed and done what you pleased. And I did get that phone call.'' A hint of reprimand entered his voice. ''I have always worried about the company you choose to keep. I suppose it must have been some man you met on your travels who took you captive.'' His gaze swung to Lance. ''Have you caught up with him yet?''

Victoria flushed with rage. He'd made her sound like a trollop who picked up men in pubs or wherever she could find them. ''My friends have always been good, decent people. And it wasn't any stranger I met on my trip who abducted me.''

Ignoring her disclaimer as if it were a childish cry of innocence, Malcolm concentrated on Lance. ''Have you caught the man responsible for my daughter's abduction?''

Lance saw through Malcolm's ploy. The man was trying to paint Victoria as a loose woman who attracted the wrong kind of men. It took all of his willpower not to come to her defense and reveal the contempt he was feeling toward Rockford. But this was Victoria's game and he would let her play it out. ''No, we have not captured those responsible yet.''

Victoria looked to Captain Grayson. She couldn't tell if he believed Malcolm's description of her or not. Her embarrassment turned to outrage that Malcolm would stoop so low as to demean her unfairly. In case they had misjudged him and he honestly did not know of her parentage, she had planned to break the news with some subtlety. Now she had no such qualms. "I was kidnapped because you are not my father. My real father is Victor Thorton."

Malcolm's gaze jerked to her. His hands went to his chest and he took a step back as if he'd just been punched. "The Grand Duke? Your father? I don't believe it. Maribelle deceived me?" His shoulders sagged and in a voice close to a whisper he said, "I can't believe this."

Victoria was surprised by Malcolm's reaction. She'd never seen him so animated. But she couldn't be certain he was acting. For her part, as she'd delivered the news to him, she'd found herself still having some difficulty believing it and she'd actually met with the Grand Duke and Duchess.

For a long moment, Malcolm was silent as if he needed time for this information to sink in, then he turned his gaze to Lance. "Is what Victoria says really true?"

"Yes."

Malcolm sank into a chair. Looking up at Victoria, he asked, "How long have you known?"

"After I was rescued, Captain Grayson told me."

Comradeship entered Malcolm's voice. "It would appear that your mother deceived us both."

Cynical amusement swept through Victoria. After a lifetime of making her feel like less than the dirt under his feet, he was trying to unite her with him against her mother. "She made a mistake, but she tried very hard to be a good wife to you and a good mother to me."

"Yes. Yes, of course, she did," Malcolm conceded, continuing to sound like a man numbed by an unexpected blow. "I'm just having some difficulty adjusting to this information."

"You honestly had no clue that I wasn't really your daughter?" she demanded skeptically.

"I suppose down deep I suspected that might be the case. You were a fairly good-size baby for one who was supposed to be so premature. But I didn't want to acknowledge that possibility. I loved your mother. I didn't want to even consider the possibility that she would deceive me in such a hurtful manner."

Victoria was having a very difficult time viewing Malcolm as a victim. "I find it hard to believe you didn't guess. You treated me as if you found my presence in your home distasteful."

"That is totally unfair. You were a difficult child. I was merely attempting to fulfill my parental obligation to form you into a good person."

"By making me feel bad about myself?" she seethed.

"Your mother had a tendency to spoil you." Again a stricken look came over his features. "Now I understand why." A plea for understanding entered his voice. "I felt it was up to me to undo the damage she was causing. Even if it alienated you, I could not in good conscience shirk my duty as a parent."

Malcolm had always had a logical answer for any

accusation she'd ever thrown at him. Still, he did look like a man whose world had come crumbling down around him. Abruptly, she reminded herself that he hadn't treated her sister the way he had treated her. "You were always kind to Rachel."

"Your sister was a much more amiable child. She needed only a quick glance of reprimand to put her back on the straight and narrow." Leaning forward, Malcolm rested his elbows on his knees and held his head in his hands. "This is such a shock. I trusted your mother and loved her dearly. How could she betray me like this?"

Victoria remained uncertain what to believe. Rachel had been a very sweet child and maybe she, Victoria, had had a little too much vinegar. Perhaps she had misjudged Malcolm. "I'm sure Mother never meant to cause you pain."

Lance was amazed that she could show compassion for this man. He just hoped it wasn't misplaced. He'd known sociopaths who could lie so convincingly they could fool the Pope. Malcolm Rockford fit that mold.

A bitter smile tilted one corner of Malcolm's mouth. "I suppose her betrayal isn't as difficult for you as it is for me. Discovering that you're a princess must have taken some of the sting off."

Rebellion swelled within Victoria. He was trying to make her feel guilty for not siding with him against her mother. "My being a princess has come very close to getting me killed."

He grimaced with sympathy. "It would appear we must all pay a price for your mother's deception."

Victoria studied him narrowly. Nothing he had said or done so far was totally out of character. Well, the smile and hug were a bit unusual. But his attempt to pit her with him against her mother was what she would have expected. Pitting people against each other was one of his usual ploys, one he'd always been good at. *Consider the evidence,* she ordered herself. "You were the only one who knew my actual travel plans. In fact, you demanded that I keep you informed and tell you if they should change."

Malcolm looked surprised at her abrupt change in subject. Rising, he approached her and clasped her hands in his. "I was concerned about you. You took your mother's death very hard."

Again Lance's protective instincts rebelled against the man touching Victoria, and it took all of his control to keep from stepping between them.

Victoria was as startled by Malcolm's fatherly gesture of holding her hands as she had been when he'd hugged her. In all of her youth, he'd avoided any physical contact with her. Then she saw it...the very, very slight tightening of his jaw that always occurred when he was forced to do something he found distasteful. In that moment, she knew he hated her enough to be involved in her kidnapping. She jerked her hands free as accusation spread over her face. "While I was away, I called and let you know where I was at various times and when I was coming home because I thought that, with my mother gone, you felt lost and alone and were turning to me for some kind of connection. I knew we could never be close, but I felt I should try to offer some solace. You were, as far as I knew, my father."

"I was feeling alone," he declared. "And in spite of our differences, I was hoping you and I could become friends. Perhaps I was a little harder on you than I should have been. To be honest, I think I was jealous of your closeness with your mother."

Victoria couldn't believe her ears. Malcolm was admitting to a flaw in his character. Her mind flashed back to the days following her mother's death. He had been his usual distant, cold self. "I saw no signs, other than your insistence that I keep you posted on my itinerary, that you cared the least little bit about me."

"I find it difficult to be demonstrative."

"You've never found it difficult to demonstrate your dislike of me," she spat back acidly.

"You're overwrought," he admonished. "You've always had a tendency to be overly dramatic and you never liked being disciplined. This is the child in you talking. It's time for you to grow up."

This was the Malcolm she knew well. He was trying to undermine her self-confidence, make her feel uncertain. Well, this time it wouldn't work. "I think you've known all along about my parentage and you were involved in my kidnapping. I think, in your own twisted way, you may have loved my mother or maybe you never loved her, but simply wanted to possess her. I'm not certain you're actually capable of love. Anyway, you bided your time and when she died, you were free to seek revenge against the Grand Duke through me."

Good girl, Lance applauded. *Don't let him fool you.*

Malcolm's expression became an exaggeration of a man wrongly accused. "That's absurd."

Victoria recognized this false facade. She'd seen him turn it off and on at will many times. "I've never known you to forget or forgive a slight. I must have been a constant reminder to you of my mother's betrayal. That would explain why you've always disliked me."

"I've never disliked you. Like I tried to explain to you, you were a difficult child and your mother tended to spoil you. I was merely attempting to mold you into a better human being. Clearly, my attempts were thwarted because of your heredity. Your mother was morally flawed and the taint was born in you."

Victoria flushed with rage. "No one is perfect, but in a contest to see which one of us is more morally flawed, I'll wager you would win hands down."

Silently, Lance congratulated her again.

Malcolm breathed an exaggerated sigh. "Lord, save us from thankless children."

Victoria caught the momentary hint of amusement that glistened in his eyes before they again became shuttered. He'd enjoyed attempting to debase her in front of Captain Grayson. And there was no lingering doubt in her mind that Malcolm had been involved in her kidnapping. She was certain that every word out of his mouth had been a practiced defense against any accusations she might throw at him. She also knew she would never trip him up in a verbal battle of wills. He was way too experienced. Casting him a final scowl, she strode out of the house, Lance at her side.

Chapter Seven

As Victoria and Lance continued toward his car, she said evenly, "I have never behaved imprudently where men are concerned. And I wasn't a difficult, spoilt child."

"I believe you." Lance surprised himself by how completely he did trust her honesty. There was no one else he could name whose integrity his in-grained cynicism didn't question at least a little.

She looked up at him and smiled. A warmth spread through him and one corner of his mouth quirked upward in a crooked grin.

"A little more practice and you might actually be able to form a full smile," she teased.

Lance felt himself being drawn into the blue depths of her eyes. A softness like a gentle caress spread through him and with it came a sense of joy he'd never experienced before.

Victoria continued walking, but with her gaze locked with his, she missed her footing and tripped.

The spell Lance had been under was broken abruptly when Victoria started to fall. Catching her before she hit the ground, he heard the buzzing sound of a bullet followed by a thud as the small missile impacted with a tree. Immediately he grabbed Victoria. "Sniper fire!" he yelled to his men, racing with her to his car.

By the time they reached the vehicle, his men were surrounding both of them, blocking Victoria from a clear shot by the sniper. Once she was safely inside the car, Lance ordered her to duck down out of sight. Next he instructed his men to scour the area and write down the names of every person they encountered. "And find the bullet," he finished, climbing behind the wheel.

Speeding out of town, he cursed himself silently for letting down his guard and nearly allowing Victoria to get killed. He would not weaken like that again.

Her eyes came back to haunt him. *She'll soon be mingling with the royals and will forget I even exist,* he told himself curtly. He had a lifetime of experience to prove that would be true. His jaw hardened and he concentrated on his duty.

"Can I sit up now?" she asked, breaking the heavy silence within the car.

Lance again checked to make certain they were not being followed, then said, "Yes."

As she straightened in her seat, he noticed her hands were shaking.

"Someone actually shot at me," she said, as the full impact of what had happened hit her. "Someone actually tried to kill me."

"It's my guess that The Whisperer was afraid you'll remember something that will identify him."

"I know he wasn't Malcolm, but I am certain Malcolm was involved."

"And I'm certain that Malcolm's accomplice is someone local, someone you know, someone who's afraid that the next time you see him on the street you'll realize he's The Whisperer." His frown deepened. "I wonder if the quarrel between Malcolm and Crenshaw was staged so that we wouldn't suspect Crenshaw."

"That's possible," Victoria conceded. "Lloyd knows I can't stand him. There is no love lost between us. If he wasn't a policeman..." She let the thought trail off as another shudder shook her. Looking gratefully at the man beside her, she said, "Thank you for saving my life a second time."

Lance continued to stare grimly out the windshield. "I should never have allowed you to visit Rockford in the first place. From now on, I make the rules."

His stern command brought a soft grin to her face. "Yes, sir, Captain, sir."

Her easy acquiescence caused Lance to glance toward her. "I mean it," he stated curtly.

She continued to smile softly at him. "You have my word. You're the boss."

The gentle expression on her face made him uneasy. She looked much too bedable. *She will never belong in your bed,* he growled at himself. Love did not exist for him. Duty was the driving force in his life. And his duty was to protect the princess and return her to the Grand Duke in the same pure state in which he'd found her.

They were about halfway to Lance's cottage when Victoria's stomach growled embarrassingly loudly. "I really need something to eat," she said.

Lance checked his rearview mirror. There was no indication that anyone was following them. Ahead was a crossroads with a sign giving the distances to the towns in all directions. "We'll detour to Valeshire. It's only five miles out of our way and there's a pub there that makes good sandwiches."

Once they arrived at the pub, he chose a booth in a far corner but with a view of the door. "Scoot in," he instructed Victoria, then sat down beside her.

She knew he chose to remain close to her only so he could better protect her, but his reasons didn't matter. "Cozy," she said, letting her arm rest against his.

"Scoot farther into the corner," he ordered. "I want you as far out of sight as possible."

She noticed that he remained at the other end of their seat, keeping as much distance between them as possible. And she'd been aware that from the moment he realized she'd been shot at, his cold, insular manner had returned. Even when she'd agreed to do his bidding without a moment's hesitation, his manner hadn't softened. The cold soldier had again won his battle to dominate over the inner self he was so determined to keep hidden from the world. Studying his stern profile, she saw both sides of him...the inner man who was afraid to allow himself to care too deeply for anyone, and the outer man who would give his life to protect her. She had to admit she was beginning to like *both* of them very much.

"I think you're afraid of me," she challenged. "You're worried that I'll break through that shell of yours."

He scowled at her. "This isn't a game. I'm trying to keep you alive. You distracted me once today and nearly got yourself killed."

Victoria grinned. "So you admit I am a distraction. A pleasant one, I hope."

"A disquieting one."

His stiff tone implied he had not enjoyed the momentary diversion, but she recalled the inviting depths of his eyes. "I think you like me."

His gaze narrowed on her. "How I feel about you is of no consequence."

"I think it is of great consequence," she returned. "Because I like you." She was a little surprised by her forwardness, but Lance Grayson, she knew, was not a man subtle flirting would work with.

"You like me because I'm your protector. Once you're safe, you'll discover that you find my presence boring."

"I can't imagine ever considering your presence boring."

"Once the Grand Duke has officially recognized you and presented you, you'll be courted by royals from all over Europe."

"I doubt there will be many who would want to wed or even be seen with someone of my background."

"The only part of your background that will matter will be who sired you. Once you take the name of Thorton, all else will be erased as far as the rest of the royals are concerned."

She gave him an impatient look. "Even if no one shows disapproval to my face, they'll whisper it behind my back."

He shrugged. "Those who would hold the circumstances of your birth against you are not people you would want to associate with anyway. More to the point, the Grand Duke is a very wealthy man. When he claims you, his money alone will buy you acceptance from most."

He was right. But she didn't really care about the others. He was the only one who interested her.

The waitress approached to take their order, stopping any further exchange.

When they were alone again, Lance placed a call to his men. They had traced the line of the bullet to the upper window of a house near Rockford's. The occupants were away on vacation and the back door had been jimmied. No evidence had been left behind except for the open window. His men were still canvassing the neighborhood to find out who was home and if they'd seen anyone.

"The shot was fired from the Grangers' house?" Victoria asked when he finished relaying the information to her.

"Yes."

"You're mulling over something."

He glanced at her. She was right. The suspicion he'd had earlier was getting stronger. But, until her, no one had ever been able to tell when something was bothering him unless he wanted them to. She was a definite threat to his peace of mind. "I'm beginning to think it could be someone on the inside. When your kidnapper didn't return to the cabin, I assumed it was because he never planned to go back. The drop was the next morning and he could have been planning to either tell us where you were after he picked up the money or leave you there to die. But when he didn't show up at the drop, I began to suspect that your kidnapper knew you'd been rescued and the only way he could know is if he was involved in the operation or had a close connection to it. We purposely didn't pick up Malcolm for questioning until after the drop time so that he wouldn't know we had found you."

"So Malcolm couldn't have warned his accomplice," she muttered.

"My men can't be involved because I know where each was when you were kidnapped. But as soon as you were rescued, we did alert the Thortonburg police to maximize our manpower for the drop. I wanted to make certain the kidnapper would have no way to escape our trap." Lance paused, then continued, "Today I wanted all of my men at Malcolm's place to protect you, so I called in the ones I had at the police station going over what meager information we've been able to gather. When I ordered them to aid in setting up a protective perimeter around Malcolm's place, I made it clear I didn't want them telling the local police what they were up to. And I didn't give any of my men more than fifteen minutes notice. That means that whoever took the shot at you had to be in a position where he could observe their activities closely."

"And he'd have to know that the Grangers were out of town." Victoria was getting a very queasy feeling in the pit of her stomach. "The Grangers always inform the police when they're going to be away so that whoever is on patrol will know that if they see any activity at the place, they need to check on it."

Lance was silent for a moment, then said, "Lloyd

Crenshaw is beginning to look like a prime suspect. Do you think his services could be bought?''

Crenshaw's sneering face filled Victoria's mind and she found herself nodding in the affirmative. "In spite of the fact that he's a police sergeant, deep down I've never really trusted him. And I know he doesn't like me. Even though I never gave him any encouragement he asked me out a couple of times. I refused. After that, he always had some barb to toss my way when we met. I don't think kidnapping *me* would have bothered him one little bit.''

"My men should have information on Crenshaw—particularly whether he smokes and wears a ring—by the time we get back to the cottage.''

Victoria's food had lost its flavor. She'd been trying to remember everything she could about Lloyd Crenshaw and she'd remembered some very important details. "Crenshaw smokes and he wears a class ring. He also matches the physical description of The Whisperer. He could easily have been my captor.''

Lance placed another call to his men and ordered Crenshaw picked up for questioning. He also ordered them to check the man's record and find out what they could about him. A few minutes later, his call was returned.

"Damn!'' he cursed as he hung up.

Victoria had heard his side of the conversation. When he ordered his men to do everything they could to locate the man, she knew Crenshaw had flown the coop.

"Right after the sniper incident, he called in to the station, told his superior that he'd had a family emergency and asked for a few days off. His superior granted the time without asking any further questions so we can't immediately check up on his story. But I've got my men looking for him."

Victoria shivered. "Just the thought of that man's hands on me makes me ill."

"If he was your captor, I'll bring him to justice."

Victoria saw the glimmer of protectiveness in the cool depths of his eyes and the chill was replaced by a soft warmth.

Chapter Eight

Victoria breathed a sigh of pleasure when they parked in front of Lance Grayson's cottage. It felt like home. Surprised by how attached she'd gotten to the place, she realized that the fact it was his home was what made it feel so appealing. In spite of all the other concerns she had to occupy her thoughts, he was in the forefront of her mind most of the time. And even though he worked very hard to keep her at a distance, she found his company both soothing and stimulating.

Having feelings for him beyond friendship isn't smart, she warned herself. There was a strong possibility that she would never be able to break down the barrier he kept around his heart. *So I just don't let myself actually fall in love with him,* she reasoned. And he could be right. She could simply feel drawn to him because she saw him as her protector and when she no longer required his protection, her feelings would lessen. He most certainly wasn't the kind of man she'd pictured herself falling in love with. She wanted someone more open, more tender, more romantic.

"So what now?" she asked as they went inside.

"We wait for Crenshaw to be found."

"What if he isn't the sniper?"

"Then we keep looking until we find whoever is."

Recalling how close the bullet had come to both of them, she felt a rush of panic not only for herself but for him. "And what if the sniper finds us first?"

"No one knows about this place...not my men, no one. And I'm sending a team to a decoy estate. If my plan works, the sniper will follow them and get snared in the trap they're going to set."

Victoria visualized The Whisperer being captured and smiled. "Good."

"With any luck you'll be free to go live in the castle very soon." This thought was supposed to bring a sense of relief. Instead, he experienced a twinge of regret. Determinedly, he ignored it.

"I'll miss this cottage," she said honestly. "I've grown very fond of it."

He was aware of what rooms had been prepared for her at the castle and the luxuries that awaited her. "I'm sure once you see your quarters in the castle, you won't give this place a second thought."

"But if I do, may I come back and visit?" she persisted.

The sudden thought of this cottage without her caused a wave of loneliness as intense as that he'd felt as a child in the orphanage whenever someone he'd grown close to left. Anger at himself for allowing her to touch him so deeply welled within him. "I don't think that would be wise."

Victoria frowned. "You're a very determined man, but I'm a very determined woman. I will be your friend."

The desire to have her for a friend—or more—was strong. *She'll have no time for you once she becomes a proclaimed royal,* he mocked himself. "Do not make vows you will not keep," he said curtly, then strode toward his study.

Victoria followed. At the door of his study, she stopped and waited until he turned to face her. "I never make vows I don't keep," she assured him, then continued on to her room.

Lance stared at the space where she had stood. He'd learned life's lessons the hard way, and the one lesson he would never forget was not to let anyone get too close. Her blue eyes haunted him. Pushing her image from his mind, he phoned his men and set the trap.

In her room, Victoria sat cross-legged on the bed going through the photo album memorizing the names and faces. But always in the back of her mind was Captain Grayson's image. A smile curled her lips. He would not be rid of her so easily. He lived in the castle, too. And she would prove to him that she would always be his friend.

The thought that she would like to be much more than a friend caused her blood to race faster. "You've already determined that could be asking for trouble," she admonished herself. In the first place, he was determined never to fall in love. Just getting him to allow her to be his friend was proving nearly impossible. In the second place, her whole world had turned topsy-turvy. She shouldn't be trusting her emotions at this moment.

Pushing her muddled thoughts about Captain Grayson aside, she forced herself to return to memorizing names and faces.

The next afternoon, Victoria was foraging around in the refrigerator and cabinets when Lance entered the kitchen. "What are you looking for?" he asked.

"Something to make you a home-cooked meal with," she replied. "You don't have a great selection, but I think I've found enough ingredients to make something cheesy with vegetables and pasta."

That she refused to understand they could not be friends made him tense. He'd never met anyone as persistent as her. And he'd never seen a woman look so endearingly domestic. "There is no reason for you to cook for me."

She grinned up at him. "Then I'll cook for me and you may share."

Shaking his head, he left the kitchen. *She's a princess and as soon as she steps into that position, she'll lose all interest in me,* he again told himself. Silently, he prayed that Crenshaw would be caught soon so she could start down the path that lay ahead of her…a path on which he would be only a shadow in the background.

"Dinner is served," Victoria informed him from the doorway of his study.

Lance had been trying not to think about how the aroma of her cooking made this place feel like the home he'd always wanted but had never had. Rising, he followed her back to the kitchen. The candles she'd lit created a romantic atmosphere that made him uneasy. He found her much too appealing as it was. Just sitting at the same table with her stirred feelings he was having trouble keeping buried. He didn't need candlelight making her eyes seem even bluer and highlighting the luster of her dark hair. "I'm waiting for a call. I'll take mine back to the study," he said, picking up his plate and departing.

In the next instant, Victoria was striding after him. "Haven't you ever heard that no man is an island," she demanded. "I can't believe you're not lonely in that solitary cell you've built around yourself."

He turned to face her. "I am, but I'd rather be lonely than disappointed."

"I won't disappoint you."

The control Lance had been holding over himself

broke. Setting his plate on the hall table, he closed the distance between them in one long stride. "You could prove to be the biggest disappointment of my life." His hands closed around her upper arms. Lifting her toward him, he found her mouth.

He had never dreamed a woman could taste so good. With every fiber of his being he wanted to claim her for his own. *She will leave you,* his inner voice warned. Just the thought caused so intense a pain, he winced. Breaking the contact, he stepped back and released his hold. "That should never have happened. I apologize," he said stiffly.

"I didn't mind." Victoria was amazed she could speak, her body was still tingling with sensations that made her feel more alive than she'd ever felt.

She thought she'd been kissed before. Now she knew she was wrong. His lips on hers had been hungry and awakened a hunger within her more intense than any she'd ever experienced. Fire had flowed from his touch, heating her blood.

"It will not happen again." This vow, it seemed, was made as much to himself as to her.

She studied his shuttered features, searching for some sign of emotion. His jaw twitched ever so slightly and she knew his control was costing him greatly. One corner of her mouth curled into a crooked smile. "I would really regret that."

"You have a whole new life ahead of you. When you are free to pursue it, you will be grateful that I behaved with honor." Turning on his heels, he retrieved his dinner and went into the study.

Following him, she stood in the door of the study and watched him sit down at his desk, then said honestly, "You affect me in a way I've never been affected before. I might actually have allowed you to ravish me. And we both might have regretted that later. I certainly don't want to end up the way my mother did...pregnant and having to marry the wrong man. But it is very possible that you are the right man for me. Very, very possible. And I'd like to find out."

Lance studied her. She looked so truthful, he nearly weakened again. Curtly he forced himself to draw up the images of his childhood and the barrier he kept around himself again became strong. "You are merely expressing gratitude for my having saved your life," he repeated what he was certain was the truth. "When this is over, you will gladly bid me goodbye and find more interesting companions."

"This feels like a lot more than gratitude."

His jaw tensed. "That is all it is."

She approached the desk and kissed him lightly on the forehead. "If you say so," she said with a smile that mocked his words, then strolled out.

Lance's jaw clenched as the residual heat of her kiss spread through him. *She's a princess and the Grand Duke has plans for her to marry royalty,* he reminded himself tersely. He would do nothing to mar her future.

* * *

As Victoria returned to the kitchen, embers of desire continued to burn within her and the memory of his kiss was so strong, she could still feel his lips on hers. They had known each other a very short while and she'd never believed in love at first sight. But then she hadn't fallen in love with him at first sight. She hadn't even trusted him at first. Now she trusted him completely. And, if what she was feeling now wasn't love, it was an animal magnetism that was so intense, she hungered for the mere sight of him.

Seating herself at the table, she stared at the flickering flame of the candle. "So what do I do?" she murmured.

"I've decided to take that decision out of your hands," a voice said in hushed tones.

Fear paralyzed her. It was The Whisperer. He'd found her. Her gaze swung in the direction from which the voice had come.

Crenshaw stepped out of his hiding place near the back door, a gun with a silencer leveled at her.

Disgust caused her skin to prickle. "So it was you."

"You should have treated me more nicely. If you had, I might have had second thoughts when Malcolm told me of his plan." He screwed his face into a mocking grimace that made him look even more ratlike than usual. "On the other hand, there was so much money involved, I probably would have done it anyway.'' Anger verging on rage replaced the mocking grimace. ''But that sister of yours had to get involved and then Captain Grayson. After I take care of you, I'll make them pay. I hate having my plans spoilt.''

Panic for Rachel and Lance replaced her fear for herself. ''I don't think Malcolm will approve of you harming Rachel.''

''I don't give a damn what Malcolm would or would not approve. I'm the one who has to clean up this mess and there won't be even one penny in it.'' He raised the gun for a better aim.

Victoria's hands had been resting in her lap. In one swift movement, she lifted the table, pushing it over on one side and ducking behind it. Her plate, the candle, the serving dish and everything else crashed to the floor while she screamed at the top of her lungs, ''Crenshaw's here and he's armed.''

A bullet pierced the wood of the table and whizzed by her shoulder.

''Damn you,'' Crenshaw cursed, moving closer for a better shot.

Keeping out of his sight, Victoria scooted down to the far end of the table.

Hearing the crash followed by Victoria's shouted warning, Lance raced toward the kitchen, pulling his gun from its holster as he sped to her rescue. He had never felt so frantic. Reaching the kitchen door, he stood to one side and pushed it open. A bullet whooshed into the hall, hitting the wall across from him.

Dropping low, he stepped into the doorway. Crenshaw was standing barely three feet from where Victoria cowered behind the table. Lance fired at Crenshaw's chest. Crenshaw cursed and fired back.

Lance felt pain rip through his chest. He ignored it. Stunned that Crenshaw hadn't gone down with his first shot, he saw the man was wearing a bullet-proof vest. He aimed for Crenshaw's gun arm and fired. Crenshaw let out a shriek, letting Lance know the bullet had hit. As Crenshaw's arm went limp, Lance fired again, this time at Crenshaw's leg. Crenshaw crumpled to the floor.

Victoria was out of her hiding place in an instant. Crenshaw was clutching his leg and she grabbed up his gun from where he'd dropped it. "Worm!" she seethed.

"Is Malcolm anywhere in the vicinity?" Lance demanded, glaring down at Crenshaw.

"You think he'd actually do any of the dirty work himself?" Crenshaw spat back, his tone letting them know that Malcolm was nowhere near.

"How did you find this place?" Lance growled.

Victoria heard the pain in his voice. Looking at him, she saw the circle of red growing larger and larger on his shirt. "You're hurt." Terror for him flowed through her.

Sinking to his knees, he said, "My handcuffs are in the study. Get them. There's also a sheet of paper on my desk that has the coordinates of this place. Call the number at the top of the sheet. One of my men will answer. Tell them to get here on the double.''

Victoria saw him weakening by the second and knew she had very little time. Running to the study, she punched in the number with trembling fingers and relayed the information. It took less than a minute, but seemed like an hour. Grabbing the handcuffs, she raced back to the kitchen.

"Put them on him," Lance directed.

"I'm bleeding here and you want to handcuff me?" Crenshaw protested.

Victoria ignored the man and did as she was told.

"Keep his gun on him until my men arrive," Lance barely got out before he slumped to the ground and lost consciousness.

Keeping the gun on Crenshaw, Victoria hurried to Lance's side. "Don't you dare die on me," she said, kneeling beside him. Grabbing up the tablecloth, she pressed it hard against his wound, trying to staunch the flow of blood.

From outside she heard the sound of a helicopter. "Hurry. Hurry," she murmured frantically.

The door burst open moments later and four men entered the room. Two went to Crenshaw. The other two hurried to her. "Captain Grayson is seriously wounded," she said around the lump in her throat. In a voice that held no compromise, she added, "You've got to help him."

One of the men was carrying a medical kit. He took one look at Lance and said, "This is a load-and-carry. I can't do anything for him here."

"What about me?" Crenshaw yelled. "You can't just let me bleed to death."

"You're going to live," one of the men kneeling beside him said, as he began to bind the wounds to cut down on the bleeding. "Nothing important got hit."

Victoria barely heard the exchange. Her full attention was on Lance. The two men by his side had not waited for a stretcher. One had lifted him by his shoulders and the other by his legs and they were carrying him as fast as they could toward the helicopter on the beach. Staying with them, she watched as they loaded him inside. "I'm coming with you," she said, climbing in and kneeling beside him.

The medic gave the pilot a nod and they took off as a second helicopter landed. Below, she saw Crenshaw being carried out of the house, then everything was forgotten but the man lying on the floor of the helicopter.

"How bad is it?" she managed to choke out.

"Can't tell for sure," the medic replied. "Collapsed lung probably. Maybe more damage." He gave her an encouraging look. "Captain Grayson's as tough as they come."

Victoria was too afraid to reply. She felt as if a part of her was lying there. Clasping his hand tightly in hers, she leaned close to his ear. "Don't you dare leave me."

He gave no sign that he heard and the hot tears welling in her eyes flowed over and down her cheeks.

The next minutes were a blur. The helicopter landed at the hospital in Thortonburg and a crew of white-coated attendants raced out with a gurney. Lance was loaded onto it in a flash and ushered inside. Victoria followed. A doctor began issuing orders and someone yelled that the operating room was ready.

One of the men who had arrived with the helicopter took her by the arm. "I'm Hardcort, Your Highness, with the royal security detail. Please, come with me. It's not safe for you to be so exposed."

"I want to stay with him," she protested. In the back of her mind, she knew she couldn't. Still, she was afraid to let him out of her sight for fear she would never see him again.

"We have to let the doctors work," Hardcort said with gentle insistence. "And we need to get you to the castle."

"No." Victoria jerked free. "I'm not leaving until I know Captain Grayson is going to be all right."

Hardcort frowned. "He'll have all of our heads if anything happens to you."

Victoria stood her ground. "I'm not leaving."

For a long moment, Hardcort hesitated, then said

reluctantly, "There's a private waiting room on the surgical floor where you can wait."

Nodding her agreement, she allowed him to escort her to an elevator. As they entered, she heard Crenshaw demanding immediate medical attention. Rage toward the man swept through her. Then Malcolm's image filled her mind. "Crenshaw admitted that Malcolm planned my kidnapping," she told Hardcort.

He punched a button on his walkie-talkie. "Have Rockford picked up. We don't want him getting wind of this and slipping through our fingers."

"How did Crenshaw find us?" Victoria asked.

Hardcort punched the button on his intercom a second time and relayed her question. They had been in the waiting room for a few minutes when another of Lance's men joined them. Hardcort introduced him as Glades.

Glades bowed, then said, "Crenshaw knew from rumors at the police precinct that Captain Grayson had taken it upon himself to personally see to your safety and figured he could trace your whereabouts through the captain. So he gave Malcolm a tracking device to stick to your clothes in the very likely event that you would confront him. The shots fired at you and Captain Grayson weren't meant to kill, but to force you back to the safe house where there wouldn't be so many from the security detail present. I personally think Crenshaw enjoyed watching your reaction."

"Thank you, Sergeant," Hardcort said with dismissal.

Glades gave a snappy salute and left.

"Can I get you some coffee?" Hardcort offered.

"No, thanks," Victoria replied, staring at the door and willing a doctor to enter and tell her that Lance was going to be all right. But no one came.

Nearly an hour later, she was pacing the floor and still waiting for news, when the Grand Duke and Duchess entered. Horror spread over their faces.

"You've been hurt and no one has tended to you?" Victor demanded, his gaze resting accusingly on Hardcort.

Victoria looked down at herself and realized she had Lance's blood on her clothes. "I'm fine. I was uninjured. This is Captain Grayson's blood. He saved my life."

"For which he will be rewarded," Victor declared. Reprimand toward Hardcort continued to show on his face for another long moment, then fatherly concern filled his voice as he turned back to her. "But you should have been taken to the castle immediately. You've been through a horrible ordeal. You need to clean up and rest."

Not wanting to get Lance's men into trouble, she said, "Hardcort wanted to escort me to the castle, but I refused to leave until I was assured Captain Grayson was going to be all right."

"My dear, you must brace yourself for the worst. He was very badly injured," Victor said gently.

For a long moment, Victoria was mute with panic. Finally she was able to make her vocal cords work. "You have heard something of his condition? They have told us nothing."

He draped an arm around her shoulders. "I spoke with a nurse before I joined you."

His tone told her the prognosis wasn't good. Tears again filled her eyes. "He can't die. I owe him my life. I have to thank him."

"It was his duty to protect you. He is a man of honor and will be glad to have died doing his duty."

Her jaw hardened. "He can't die." In the next instant, her jaw trembled. He could and she knew it. The image of the little boy who had been deserted his whole life came strongly into her mind. "He has no one. I won't let him die alone."

"Yes, of course you must stay." The Duchess approached and took her hands in a motherly fashion. "We are aware that he has no family. And he shouldn't be alone."

Victoria saw the sincere concern in Sara's eyes and knew Sara realized how much Lance had come to mean to her. "Thank you."

Sara smiled and gave her hands a gentle squeeze before releasing them. Then looking to her husband she said, "We will wait with Victoria."

Victor nodded his consent. Guiding Sara to one of the couches, he motioned for her to be seated, then seated himself.

Victoria knew from Sara's manner that neither

she nor Victor expected Lance to live and wanted
to be there to comfort Victoria when the news of his
death was delivered. The Grand Duchess was living
up to her words. She did want to be Victoria's friend
and a mother figure. This knowledge should have
brought relief, but Victoria could feel nothing but
fear for Lance.

He will live! she repeated over and over again in
her mind as if by sheer willpower she could make
it so.

Chapter Nine

Victoria sat by Lance's bedside in the intensive care unit. Even after he'd survived the operation, she'd refused to leave the hospital. She wanted to be there when he first regained consciousness so that he would know she had not left him. In the end, with worried blessings, the Grand Duke and Duchess had left without her.

Her suitcases had been flown to the castle soon after she'd arrived at the hospital. Upon Sara's return to the castle, she sent fresh garments to Victoria. Victoria had showered and changed at the hospital, then resumed her sentry duty at Lance's bedside.

The doctors assured her that he was a strong man, and because he'd survived the operation, they had every hope he would be fine. Still, her fears remained. Holding his hand in both of hers, she tried to will her own strength into him.

A low moan from the bed brought her to her feet. "Lance, it's Victoria. You're going to be just fine."

Lance opened his eyes a slit. He had trouble forming words. "Princess, did Crenshaw hurt you?" he murmured in a harsh whisper.

A hint of a smile curled the corners of her mouth. Even in his weakened state, she heard the promise of retribution in his voice. "No. I'm fine," she assured him.

Fear for her showed on his face. "What about the others involved? Did Crenshaw talk? Are they behind bars?"

"Yes, it's over. Crenshaw has been singing like a bird, trying to work out some sort of a deal for a lesser sentence. His confession makes it clear that it was only Malcolm and him involved."

Satisfied, he closed his eyes and lapsed into unconsciousness.

Victoria buzzed the nurse, terror filling her as she watched the woman check Lance over.

"He's sleeping peacefully now," the nurse replied in response to her unspoken question. "You said that he was coherent when he awoke. That's a good sign. I'd say he's going to be just fine."

Victoria breathed a sigh of relief. While the nurse put in a call to the doctor, she leaned close to Lance and said softly, "I will always be here for you and don't you ever forget that."

His jaw twitched as if he'd experienced a slight discomfort.

"I hope that's a piece of that wall you keep around your heart crumbling," she murmured. Then, noting that the nurse wasn't watching, she kissed him lightly on the cheek before sitting down.

The next time Lance woke, he was in a hospital room. As his eyes focused, he saw Victoria in a nearby chair. Her presence comforted him. Even more, she made him feel wanted. A memory stirred. He heard her vowing always to be there for him. *Don't believe it,* his inner voice warned. *Most likely it was just a dream and even if it wasn't, she will not keep her word.*

Sensing that she was being watched, Victoria looked toward him and met his gaze. Her smile was one of relief. "Good morning." Her expression turning serious, she rose to stand by his bedside and took his hand in hers. "You had me scared half to death for a while."

There was a tenderness in her face that warmed him to the core. *Remember who she is,* he ordered, curtly reminding himself of the new life that lay ahead for her. "Do your quarters in the castle suit you?"

"I haven't seen them. I didn't want you to wake up alone. I want you to know that I will always be here for you."

She made him want to lower the shield he kept

around his heart, but he forced himself to recall the other times he'd let others get close. No one had ever remained at his side. "That's very kind of you, Princess. But it isn't necessary. It's time for you to put all that has happened during the past days behind you and to get on with your life."

She ignored the dismissal in his voice. "I am not leaving."

"You don't belong here."

She frowned down at him. "You're a very difficult man to get to know. You're bullheaded and stubborn. However, when you were injured, I realized a very important thing. I'm in love with you."

No one had ever said that to him. Her words crashed against his shield with threatening force. A lifetime of bitter disappointments rushed to the forefront of his mind and his instinct for survival warned him that should she prove to be insincere, the blow would wound him so deeply, it would be fatal. His shield held. "You'll get over it."

Frustration at his determined resistance showed on her face. "I am not that shallow."

"What you're feeling is gratitude and relief that you're safe." He repeated the mantra he was convinced was the truth. "Once you have begun your new life, you'll realize I'm right and be relieved I didn't take you seriously."

"I was wrong. You're not difficult, you're impossible," she grumbled. "But I can be just as strong-willed as you." Returning to her chair, she picked up the magazine she'd been reading and feigned interest in it.

Lance shifted his gaze to the ceiling and pictured her at a royal ball. *She'll have every eligible royal male courting her. I'll be forgotten in a wink of an eye,* he assured himself.

A light knock on the door pulled Victoria's attention in that direction. In the next instant she was on her feet, grinning widely as a pretty, auburn-haired woman entered the room. "Rachel," she said, rushing to give her sister a hug.

"I'm so glad that you're finally safe," Rachel said, returning the hug.

Past her sister's shoulder, Victoria saw that a man had entered as well. He was elegantly attired and had a noble air. "You must be Prince Damon Montague," she said, releasing her sister and performing a small curtsy.

"At your service, Princess." He bowed in deference to her station.

"This being a princess is going to take a little getting used to," Victoria confessed, wondering if it had been proper of her to curtsy or if she should simply have offered to shake his hand.

"You'll get used to it," Rachel assured her. Looking lovingly at Damon, she added, "At least that is what Damon tells me." Her gaze swung back to Victoria. "We asked Captain Grayson to keep our secret because we wanted to tell you ourselves."

Victoria thought her sister looked like a woman

who might burst from happiness. "What secret?" she prodded, already guessing and hoping she was right.

"Damon and I are married," Rachel said, glancing toward her husband with a loving smile.

Victoria hid her shock. She'd expected to hear that they were merely engaged. Tears of joy for her sister welled in Victoria's eyes. "I'm so very happy for you." She turned to Damon. "For both of you."

"I consider myself a very lucky man," Damon replied. Then he approached the hospital bed and said, "Thank you, Captain Grayson, for delivering Rachel's sister to safety."

Rachel, too, approached the bed. "Yes, thank you so much, Captain Grayson. I am eternally in your debt."

Obviously uncomfortable with so much praise being heaped upon him, Lance said stiffly, "I was merely doing my duty."

"Still, you have my undying gratitude," Rachel replied.

Damon shifted his attention from Captain Grayson to the women. "We have only a short time here in Thortonburg," he reminded Rachel. "The nurse said you ladies could use the room next door for a private visit."

"Yes, we must talk," Rachel said, taking Victoria's arm.

Victoria glanced back at Lance. "I'll be back," she said firmly.

* * *

Rachel waited until she and Victoria were alone in the room next to Lance's and said, "Your promise to return to the captain's room sounded like a warning. What's going on between the two of you?"

Victoria grimaced with frustration. "I'm in love with him, but he refuses to believe me. He insists that what I'm feeling is merely gratitude."

Rachel regarded her worriedly. "You've known him only a short time and under very stressful circumstances. Perhaps he's right. I've had experience with false love. It can be very deceptive."

"You know I've always been practical where love is concerned, and what happened to you and our mother has made me even more determined not to make a mistake. But I know with all my heart that loving Lance Grayson is not a mistake."

Rachel smiled. "Then I'm sure you will convince him of that." Her smile vanished abruptly and sympathy mingled with anger in her features. "I am so sorry about what Father did to you. I will never forgive him."

Victoria gave her another hug. "I'm just glad you came looking for me."

Disgust flashed in Rachel's eyes. "And Crenshaw…that ghastly man. He was the one who took my report and tried to make it sound as if you were always going off doing wild things." A softness came over her face. "But Damon came to my aid."

Not wanting to discuss Malcolm or Crenshaw,

Victoria said, "You must tell me about your prince. I recall from articles I've read about him that he is considered a very honorable man."

"Honorable and wonderful," Rachel confirmed.

Victoria smiled at her sister's joy, then memories of her own childhood caused a rush of concern for Rachel's daughter. Her expression became terse. "What of my niece Carly? How does Damon like instant fatherhood?"

Rachel gave her a reassuring smile. "Damon loves Carly and Carly adores Damon. They hit it off from the start."

Relaxing, Victoria turned the conversation back to Rachel and Damon and their plans for the future.

It was nearly an hour later that Victoria stood at the window of Lance's third-story hospital room and watched her sister and Damon walking to Damon's car. "I'm so happy Rachel was found true love," she said. Turning around she leveled her gaze at Lance. "Now all I have to do is convince you that my motives are pure."

He regarded her sagely. "Go start your new life. You'll discover there's no place for me there."

For a long moment she studied him in silence, then approached the bed. "The Grand Duke has requested my company at dinner tonight, so I will go. But I'll be back tomorrow." Leaning over the railing, she gave him a light kiss on the lips before she turned and left the room.

Watching her leave, Lance continued to feel the imprint of her lips on his. His arms ached to hold her and he wanted to believe in her love. Sending her away was the hardest thing he'd ever done, but he couldn't believe that she really loved him. No one had ever loved him. Mentally he began ticking off those who had disappointed him in the past beginning with his mother. He finished by repeating the vow he'd made to himself while still a youngster. He'd promised he would never allow himself to be hurt again by those who offered their caring then withdrew it.

As Victoria left Lance's room, Hardcort rose from the chair beside the door and snapped to attention.

"The time has come for me to go to the castle," she said.

He nodded, then pressed a button on his walkie-talkie and requested that her car be brought to the side entrance and a decoy sent to the front. "The press has gotten wind of your story. We have managed to keep them off this floor, but they're hovering around in the reception area and outside," he explained. "The decoy should keep them at the front entrance long enough for us to exit without incident."

She paled. "The press. I didn't even think about them."

Hardcort smiled. "They have painted you, and rightly so, as the heroine of the piece and Captain

Grayson as the hero. The Grand Duke has been forgiven for his youthful indiscretion because he was so willing to accept responsibility for you and send his men into the field to rescue you. There is some sympathy for the Duchess, of course, but no anger or blame directed at you because of it.''

Victoria breathed a sigh of relief. ''Thank you for that information and your support,'' she said.

He bowed low.

Walking toward the elevators, she found herself amazed by how he and others accepted her new position while she was still finding it very hard to believe.

A few minutes later, seated alone in the rear of a Rolls-Royce limousine with tinted windows, her thoughts didn't go to her arrival at the castle. Instead, she couldn't get Malcolm out of her mind. There were a couple of answers she needed. Tapping on the window that separated her from the driver and Hardcort, she got the bodyguard's attention. ''I want to stop and speak to Malcolm Rockford before we continue to the castle,'' she said.

''They are expecting you at the castle,'' he replied, clearly not wanting to fulfill her request.

''This will only take a short while. It's something I have to do,'' she insisted.

''Yes, Your Highness,'' he acquiesced reluctantly and made the arrangements.

At the prison, she was led in by a side door and taken to a nearby room. Malcolm was inside, seated in a chair, irons on his wrists and ankles. She saw hatred in his eyes.

"I suppose you've come to gloat," he said.

"I find nothing in this situation worth gloating about," she returned tersely.

He sneered with disbelief. "Then why have you come?"

"I want to know how long you've known about me."

Malice joined the hatred in his eyes. "Almost from the start. I realized on our wedding night that your mother was no virgin. But I accepted that. However, when she announced that she was pregnant and the pregnancy began to show so quickly, my suspicions grew. When you were born premature but with a good birth weight, I was almost certain you weren't mine."

"Did my mother know you knew I wasn't yours?"

"Yes, I confronted her. But she refused to name the father. I told her that if she stayed with me and behaved as a good wife should, I would raise you as my own. But if she left me, I would tell the world of her deceit."

"And thereby bring shame on her, and me," Victoria muttered dryly. "When did you learn about the Grand Duke?"

"On her deathbed your mother finally confessed. She said the birthmark you bore was proof. The Grand Duke had told her all Thortons possessed it."

Pride etched itself into his features. "She had deceived me gravely. I couldn't let that slight go without retribution."

"She not only stayed with you but she bore you a child. I would say she paid her debt to you."

"Perhaps," he conceded. "But you...you could never repay me for your presence under my roof. And the Grand Duke deserved to be punished as well."

Victoria shook her head in disgust. "And I spent so many years of my youth trying to please you, trying to make you like me." Unable to even look at him any longer, she strode to the door and knocked. It was immediately opened and she left without a backward glance.

Chapter Ten

Victoria sat on the huge, ornate, canopied bed, her arms wrapped around her legs with her chin resting on her knees. Never had she been surrounded by such luxury. Her suite consisted of five rooms...a sitting room, a study, a bedroom, a private bath and a maid's room. There were paintings by famous artists on the walls and the furniture was of the highest craftsmanship.

"Wow," she whispered, feeling the need to say something and unable to come up with anything else.

Her stomach grumbled. Glancing at the porcelain clock on the bedside table, she realized she had no time to waste if she wanted breakfast. It was already eight and the Duchess had arranged for her personal clothier, a designer by the name of Charles Tobalt, to come at nine to discuss Victoria's wardrobe.

Victoria pressed a button on the small box sitting on the bedside table and heard a soft bell ring in the distance. Upon her arrival at the castle, she'd learned that not only did her suite contain a maid's room, but a maid had been assigned to her.

Mary was in her mid-twenties, a little on the chubby side, with brown hair and eyes and a pleasant face and disposition. In only seconds Victoria's bedroom door opened.

Mary, already dressed in her uniform, entered and curtsied. "How may I serve you?"

"I'd like some breakfast," Victoria replied, then gave her selections.

As the maid scurried to obey, Victoria picked up the phone and called the hospital. Assured that Lance had had a good night and was doing well, she hung up and headed for the bathroom to shower.

Upon waking, Lance could not stop himself from immediately turning his gaze to the chair Victoria had occupied. It was empty. Scanning the rest of the room, he noted that she was not there. *She has begun her life in the castle. She has no time to sit around hospital rooms now.* Mentally he patted himself on the back. This was what he had predicted.

He had been certain he hadn't allowed her to creep into his heart. But as the morning wore on, he had to admit that her absence disturbed him. Refusing to admit that he missed her, he told himself that he still felt responsible for her and simply wanted to be assured that she was doing well.

Restless, he was glad when the nurse told him that it was time for him to get up and walk around. Ignoring the pain, he began to pace the corridor, determined to get well and out of this place as quickly as possible. Already, it felt as if the walls were closing in on him.

By noon, confined to his bed again, he was recalling with bitter cynicism the princess telling him that she was in love with him. *Good thing, I didn't believe her,* he mused acidly. Like all the others in his life who had professed to care about him, she'd walked out and never looked back.

Suddenly, he stiffened. The door of his room had opened and without even looking toward it, he knew Victoria had entered.

"I understand you're doing very well today," she said, approaching the bed.

Hardcort was with her, carrying two huge bouquets of flowers.

"Put them on the windowsill, Hardcort," she directed.

Hardcort did as instructed, then turned to the bed. "I'm pleased to see you doing so well, sir. One of the vases of flowers is from the men. They send their well-wishes."

"Thank you, Hardcort, and thank them." Lance was surprised that his men had actually purchased flowers. None had come to visit him. But then, he hadn't expected them to. He knew he was a hard taskmaster and he'd never encouraged friendship between him and them.

"Your men have a great deal of admiration and respect for you," Victoria said after Hardcort exited the room. "When I was leaving the castle today, several approached me and asked about you. I suggested that they come visit and see for themselves that you are doing well, but they said they didn't think you would appreciate that. You have apparently managed to convince everyone that you do not seek their companionship nor their friendship."

Lance refused to admit how much pleasure just seeing her gave him. "I've chosen my path and I'm happy with it."

She breathed an exaggerated sigh and shook her head with disapproval. "I refuse to allow you to end up a crotchety old hermit who scares small children with one of your 'get lost' looks."

As if a light had suddenly gone on in his brain, he realized that he was a challenge to her. That was why she persisted in pursuing him. He'd had some experience with females who considered him a challenge. After a while they'd lost interest and he assured himself that the same would happen when more interesting diversions came her way. Changing the subject from him to her, he asked, "How are your quarters in the castle?"

"It's like living in an art museum. There is actually a small collection of five Fabergé eggs on one of the little tables in my sitting room. I'm almost afraid to touch anything."

"You'll get used to it."

She smiled warmly at him. "I miss your cottage."

She sounded so sincere. His mind flashed back to the two of them there, and he recalled how she'd added a warmth to his home. *She belongs in a castle, not in a cottage.* "After a few more days in the castle, I'm sure you'll prefer it to any cottage."

Victoria shook her head, then smiled down at him. "Actually, it doesn't matter to me where I am, as long as you're there."

When she looked at him that way, it took every ounce of his control to keep the barriers around his heart from crumbling into dust. *She can do much better than you,* his inner voice reminded him curtly. And when she realized that, she'd also realize that she merely liked having him around because she saw him as her protector, and as a challenge. "You'll find others whose company will please you even better."

Victoria scowled at him in frustration. "I have never met a man who is so obstinate." Changing the subject, she said, "I met my half brothers at dinner last night."

Immediately, Lance experienced a protectiveness toward her. He knew both Rafe Thorton and his younger brother, Roland. Both were good men, but still, he found himself concerned for her welfare. "Did it go well?"

She saw the slight tick in his cheek and knew he was worried for her. She smiled. "It went very well. Both were pleasant and wished me well. They also sent their regards to you, and their thanks for saving me."

Lance relaxed. The Thorton royal family was accepting her with their usual grace and charm. Malcolm and Crenshaw were behind bars. He no longer needed to worry about her. "I'm sure you have more important things to do than remain at my bedside."

The dismissal in his voice was clear and she scowled at him. "If you keep pushing me away, I may begin to believe that I can never get through that barrier you keep around yourself and not come back."

"That would be best." Never had words hurt him more to say. But just the sight of her weakened his resolve and he was convinced that eventually she would realize she did not want a future with him.

"This is not over," she vowed. Dropping a light kiss on his lips, she left.

Lance lay, his hands balled into fists as he fought the urge to call her back. But that, he assured himself, would only be hurtful to both of them. In addition to his belief that she was merely drawn to him out of gratitude and a sense of challenge, he knew the Grand Duke was planning to find a royal husband for her. Victor wanted to make up for all that she had missed. He would not be pleased with her forming an alliance with a royal bodyguard.

Victoria was pacing her sitting room floor, trying to come up with a plan, when a knock sounded on the door. She started to answer it, when Mary came rushing out of the maid's room. Realizing she was supposed to allow Mary to open the door, Victoria stopped and waited.

After opening the door, Mary dropped into a curtsy. "Your Highness," she said, then quickly stepped back.

Sara acknowledged the maid with a smile, then continued to Victoria.

Victoria curtsied as Sara approached. "Good afternoon, Your Highness."

"I've told you that you may call me Sara, and there is no need for formalities when we're alone or in the privacy of our rooms," Sara said.

"I know," Victoria replied with apology. Her gaze swept the room. "It's just very hard to get used to all of this."

Sara smiled warmly. "You will." She seated herself. "I've come to see how your meeting with Charles Tobalt went. I hope you liked his designs. I gave him your photograph several days ago and asked him to come up with some ideas he thought might please you."

"I was very impressed," Victoria replied honestly. Charles Tobalt had shown a real flair for elegant but youthful clothing. Realizing Mary had closed the door but remained in the sitting room regarding her expectantly, Victoria suddenly remembered her manners. "Would you like some tea or coffee or something?" she offered the Duchess.

"No, nothing," Sara replied.

"You may leave us," Victoria instructed, repeating what she'd heard both Victor and Sara say when they wished to dismiss their servants.

Mary curtsied once again, then went to her room to give them privacy.

"I'm glad Charles's designs pleased you. But you must feel free to find your own designer or designers as well." Sara's smile was motherly. "Victor and I want you to feel comfortable here. To do that you will require some instruction in protocol. With your permission, I'll have Lord Proford call upon you."

"I would appreciate that," Victoria replied. "I do feel like a fish out of water."

For a moment Sara seemed hesitant, then she said, "There is one other matter I feel I should inquire about."

Victoria stiffened. Was this the beginning of problems between herself and the Duchess. "Yes."

"I understand you went to visit Captain Grayson again today. It is obvious to me that you've grown quite fond of him." Sara paused, clearly waiting for a response.

"I have," Victoria confirmed. "Very fond."

Worry showed on Sara's face. "And does he return your feelings?"

"He says not. But I believe he does."

For a long moment Sara remained silent, then said, "I'm sure some women might see him as a challenge."

Great! Just great! Victoria grumbled mentally. *Yet another reason Lance might convince himself that my motives are suspect.* "I do not view him as a challenge. I am in love with him."

"You've been through a great deal lately. Are you so very positive of your emotions? It could simply be gratitude that you feel."

"That's what he is determined to believe," Victoria replied, letting her frustration show.

"Your father had great hopes for you to marry into one of the royal families."

"I suppose my father has guessed how I feel about the captain and sent you here to talk some sense into me."

"No. He believes your affinity toward Captain Grayson is merely out of gratitude. But I can see that you've become truly attached to the captain. I simply don't want you to get hurt. Captain Grayson can be somewhat cold."

"I have seen glimpses of the man he keeps hidden. His history has taught him to distrust others. That's why he keeps himself locked behind a facade of coldness." Victoria frowned. "The problem is that he has had years of practice in keeping a shield around his heart. I'm not certain I can ever break through.''

Sara sighed a knowing sigh. "Love can be painful."

Victoria felt caught between a rock and a hard place. "I don't want to cause trouble between my father and me so soon in our relationship. But I just can't walk away from Captain Grayson. When he was shot, I felt as if a part of me had been wounded, and if he'd died, it would have been as if a part of me had died with him."

Sara nodded her head in understanding. "You do have it bad."

Victoria grimaced and nodded back.

Sara thought for a moment, then said, "As I see it, we have two lines of action we must pursue. The first is for you to convince Captain Grayson that he is in love with you and cannot live without you. The second will be to convince the Grand Duke that Captain Grayson will be a good choice of a husband for you. The first will be up to you. The second will be my responsibility."

"You'll help me?" Victoria asked in amazement. In the next instant, she was assailed by guilt. "I appreciate the offer, but I don't want to be the cause of any more trouble between you and the Grand Duke."

The Duchess smiled. "My part will be easy. Victor wants to find a way to thank Captain Grayson for saving you. I'll suggest that a knighthood is in order. I'm sure he'll agree. And then I'll suggest to him that he should allow you to choose your own husband with as little guidance from us as possible. I will point out that our sons did very well on their own and that you appear to have inherited their same good level of common sense.''

"And you think he'll allow that?" Victoria asked.

Sara's smile became confident. "Since the discovery of your existence, he has been very good about bowing to my wishes whenever possible.''

"You are most kind.''

"My husband and I spoke of love for the first time in our marriage when his affair with your mother came to light. I had loved him for a long time, but believed that while he was fond of me, he had never truly loved me. When he confessed that he had grown to love me, it was as if my whole life was filled with a newfound joy. So you see, there has been good that has come of this for me as well.''

"I am glad for you," Victoria said with a warm smile, then she sobered. "I just hope I can find a way to convince Lance Grayson that he should allow himself to love me.''

A sparkle of mischief glistened in Sara's eyes. "I have a suggestion.''

Victoria found herself liking the Grand Duchess very much. "I'd appreciate any help.''

"The captain is well acquainted with many of the royals and those he does not know personally, he knows of. I'll draw up a list of names of possible royal husbands you could say Victor is considering for you."

Understanding brought a conspiratorial grin to Victoria's lips. "Can I assume these men have flaws."

Sara regarded her sagely. "Most men do. These, however, as far as husband material goes, have more than their fair share. You will, hopefully, be able to judge the extent of Captain Grayson's feelings for you by his reactions."

Victoria realized Sara was subtly warning her that Lance might not feel as strongly about her as she did about him. She could not fault the Duchess for having doubts. But she'd experienced the passion in his kiss and seen the softness in his eyes and was determined to believe that he did love her.

Chapter Eleven

Seated in the chair beside his bed that evening, armed with a list, Victoria said, "If you continue to refuse to allow yourself to care for me, then I may be forced to find another husband. The Grand Duke is planning to do a bit of matchmaking."

The thought of her in another man's bed caused Lance's stomach to knot. *You're merely a challenge to her,* he assured himself. One day she would regret tying herself to him. He would be glad when she was someone else's wife. That would take the temptation away because he would never interfere with a person's marriage vows. Others might take them lightly, but he considered them as binding as an oath signed in blood. "I'm sure you'll find someone much more suitable than me."

She regarded him dryly. "There's just one problem with making a choice among the Grand Duke's list of suitors. While *you* insist on hiding your better attributes behind a wall of ice, I have a feeling these men will conceal their flaws behind a curtain of charm."

Mentally, Lance congratulated himself. That she was even considering looking over other prospects was proof her feelings for him did not run as deeply as she proclaimed. "You're a clever woman. You'll find a way to see behind the curtain."

"You could be of some help."

She was asking him to help her find a husband! Lance's jaw clenched as he fought to keep his anger under control. He had not believed she could be so callous. Clearly, he'd been right to guard his heart against her. "And how can I be of service?"

"Sara has provided me with a list." She read the first name.

For a moment he considered letting Victoria fend for herself, but could not. "He has two illegitimate children already. I doubt he would be faithful once married," he said tersely.

Victoria read the second name on the list.

"He has a mistress to whom he is devoted. His family has made it clear they will disown him if he marries her. However, it is necessary for him to wed to produce heirs."

"Doesn't sound like either of the first two would

be such a great catch," Victoria mused, studying him closely. She read the third name.

"He has gambled away his fortune and is looking for a wife with money to cover his debts."

She read the fourth name.

"He drinks too much."

Victoria read the fifth name on the list.

"He's wealthy, somewhat pompous but decent enough." Picturing her with the man, Lance felt as if a knife was twisting inside of him.

Watching him very closely, Victoria read the last name on the list.

Lance glowered. "He's a meek man. You could easily deceive him into thinking you truly care. No doubt within an hour, you could have him wrapped around your little finger."

Realizing that her plan had backfired and was only serving to convince him that he was right to keep his heart from her, frustration raged through her. Rising to stand by the bed, she glowered back. "You honestly think I'm serious about this list!" She crumpled it as she spoke. "I was trying to make you jealous. I wanted you to realize that you should marry me to save me from ending up like my mother...married to the wrong man and living a life of misery."

"My greatest fear is that if I do marry you, one day you'll wake up and realize that I'm the wrong man and you're miserable with me," he confessed curtly.

He had nearly said he loved her. Hope welled within her. "That will never happen."

His jaw hardened. "I'm not willing to take that chance for either of our sakes."

Victoria read the resolve on his face and her hope died. His fear of rejection was too deep and too strong. He would never give his heart to her. Unable to speak, she strode out of the room.

For a long time, Lance lay staring at the ceiling. He wanted to hold her in his arms and never let her go, but he couldn't convince himself that she truly loved him. It was much more logical to believe that her attachment to him had been born out of her gratitude to him for saving her. Once she got past the trauma of her kidnapping, she would forget him.

He envisioned her walking down the aisle, the centerpiece of a royal wedding. That, he could not witness. Reaching for the phone, he punched in a number.

Frustrated to the point of wanting to scream, Victoria rode back to the castle in silence. By the time she arrived at her suite, she had decided that only time would convince Lance Grayson that she could be trusted with his heart. She'd also decided that perhaps her absence would force him to realize how lonely his life would be without her.

For the next few days, she busied herself learning protocol and being fitted for a new wardrobe suitable to her new station in life. At the end of the week, the Grand Duke officially presented her at court. But every day had been a struggle to make herself stay away from Lance. Every day she'd awoken with the hope that he would ask for her and confess how much he missed her.

The day after she was presented at court, she was pacing the floor of her sitting room, arguing with herself about going to visit him, when Sara entered.

"There is something you should know," the Duchess said as soon as she and Victoria were alone.

Each day Victoria had called the hospital to check on Lance's condition. Each day she'd been told that he was growing stronger and stronger. In fact, he was to be discharged in a couple of days. Terror that some unexpected complication had arisen that was threatening his life caused her knees to weaken. "What?"

"Captain Grayson has resigned and the Grand Duke has accepted the resignation. The captain has already found employment in the United States as head of security for Trey Sutherland, the husband of Princess Katherine of Wynborough. When he leaves the hospital early next week, he'll come here to be knighted, then he will pack his things and leave."

"He's trying to run away. He's afraid that if he

stays, he'll be forced to admit that he loves me. I'm not going to let him get away with that."

"Perhaps," Sara said. "Or, perhaps, he's merely trying to spare you any more pain because he doesn't love you." A plea entered her voice. "You've been through a great deal. It's only natural your emotions would be all muddled. Give yourself some time to think about how you really feel."

Victoria knew Sara was trying to be kind. No one in the castle believed Lance Grayson was actually capable of loving anyone. He was aloof, a precise, professional man. But she recalled the passion of his kiss, and she could still visualize the softness in his eyes when he'd knelt in front of her. "I will consider what you have said," she replied stiffly.

"I know I can never replace your mother, but if you want to talk, I'm always available," Sara said. Then giving Victoria a hug, she left.

A few days later, Victoria stood in front of her mirror, making one final check of her attire. Lance was to be knighted within the hour and she was to attend. She hadn't heard from him since their last encounter and would have preferred to skip the proceedings today. But since she was the reason for his knighthood, that was impossible.

"You look beautiful," Mary proclaimed with approval. "You shall have no shortage of suitors."

"Thank you," Victoria replied. For the past few days, Mary had been a fairly constant companion and Victoria had learned to read her well. "Is there something else you want to say to me?"

"Captain Grayson is a fool."

Mentally, Victoria groaned. She'd suspected there had been gossip about her and Lance. Her insistence on remaining at the hospital until she knew he was on the road to recovery and her visits afterward had obviously prompted speculation. "Does everyone in the castle know of my fondness for him?"

"Most everyone," Mary conceded, then smiled brightly. "But it's understandable. He saved your life. It's only natural you'd be extra fond of him. But it's just gratitude. You'll get over it and find yourself a fine prince to marry."

Not likely, Victoria mused as she headed to the court chamber. Well, maybe they were right.

"You're looking especially radiant today," Victor said as she took her place to his right.

Sara looked around her husband and gave Victoria an encouraging smile. "Yes, very lovely."

"Thank you both," Victoria replied. She wondered if Sara had discussed her fondness for the captain with Victor. If so, her father had chosen not to speak to her about it. As for Sara, she had said nothing about Lance since informing Victoria that he was leaving. She guessed both had concluded that Victoria had decided, like the rest of the castle, that her fondness was merely an infatuation and best forgotten.

Suddenly, above the chatter, the announcement was made that Captain Grayson had arrived. As she looked toward the back of the chamber, her breath caught in her throat. He was wearing his dress uniform, and she knew she'd never seen a man look more handsome. *He doesn't want to love you!* she reminded herself curtly.

Approaching the dais, Lance steeled himself. Since his last encounter with Victoria, he had been able to think of nothing but her. He knew what he must do. Deep inside, the small boy who had learned to be afraid to show himself quivered with fear.

Reaching the dais, he knelt.

The ceremony took only a few minutes but to Lance it felt like a lifetime. Victor was effusive in his gratitude, proclaiming him a national hero and knighting him. Finally, he stood before the Grand Duke with his title of Sir. "I have one request to make," Lance said with deference.

"Yes?" Victor replied.

"I ask for your daughter's hand in marriage."

Victoria barely noticed the collective gasp from those observing. All she could do was stare at Lance in a stunned silence. Had he really said what she thought she'd heard?

Victor was momentarily shocked into silence. Finding his voice, he said, "You want to marry Victoria?" His tone implied he thought he might have misheard.

Lance's gaze shifted to her. "I love her very deeply and promise you I will always protect her and care for her."

Tears of joy welled in Victoria's eyes. She knew how difficult this was for him, but, for her love, he was willing to let the whole world see his vulnerable side.

"Let Victoria decide," Sara whispered to her husband.

"Yes. Yes. That would be the thing to do," Victor muttered, clearly glad to have this decision taken out of his hands. Turning to his daughter, he said, "Do you wish to marry Sir Grayson?"

Lance stood stiffly, barely breathing. A lifetime of distrust warning him that he could be making a tremendous fool of himself. He could have pushed her away one too many times or she could have realized, as he'd predicted, that she did not honestly love him.

"Yes, very much," Victoria managed, tears running down her cheeks.

Relief rushed through Lance, followed by a wave of joy. Never in his life had he felt this kind of happiness.

Victor smiled. "Then it's settled."

"Permission to kiss my fiancée?" Lance requested. He knew he was going to do just that with or without the Grand Duke's permission, but years of training conditioned him to ask.

"Permission granted, Sir Grayson," Victor replied.

Then everyone was forgotten as he took Victoria in his arms and claimed her mouth with a kiss that sealed their future.

* * * * *

Be sure to look for

STORKVILLE, USA,
Silhouette Romance's next in-line continuity,
on sale August-November 2000,

featuring Marie Ferrarella,
Susan Meier,
Teresa Southwick
and Karen Rose Smith.

VIRGIN BRIDES

**Join
Silhouette Romance
as the New Year brings new
virgin brides down the aisle!**

On Sale December 1999
THE BRIDAL BARGAIN
by Stella Bagwell (SR #1414)

On Sale February 2000
WAITING FOR THE WEDDING
by Carla Cassidy (SR #1426)

On Sale April 2000
HIS WILD YOUNG BRIDE
by Donna Clayton (SR #1441)

Watch for more **Virgin Brides** stories from
your favorite authors later in 2000!

VIRGIN BRIDES
only from

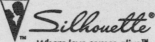

Silhouette®
Where love comes alive™

Available at your favorite retail outlet.

Visit us at www.romance.net

SRVB00

Beloved author
JOAN ELLIOTT PICKART
reprises her successful miniseries
THE BABY BET
with the following delightful stories:

On sale June 2000
TO A MacALLISTER BORN
Silhouette Special Edition® #1329
The Bachelor Bet's Jennifer Mackane proves more than
a match for marriage-wary Jack MacAllister.

On Sale July 2000
THE BABY BET: HIS SECRET SON
Silhouette Books®
A secret son stirs up trouble for patriarch
Robert MacAllister and the clan.

On sale October 2000
BABY: MacALLISTER-MADE
Silhouette Desire® #1326
A night of passion has bachelor Richard MacAllister awaiting
the next bouncing MacAllister bundle!

And coming to Special Edition® in 2001:
HER LITTLE SECRET.

Available at your favorite retail outlet.

Where love comes alive™

Visit Silhouette at www.eHarlequin.com   PSBET

Look Who's Celebrating Our 20ᵗʰ Anniversary:

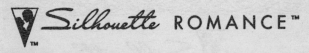

"Happy 20ᵗʰ birthday, Silhouette. You made the writing dream of hundreds of women a reality. You enabled us to give [women] the stories [they] wanted to read and helped us teach [them] about the power of love."

—*New York Times* bestselling author
Debbie Macomber

"I wish you continued success, Silhouette Books.... Thank you for giving me a chance to do what I love best in all the world."

—International bestselling author
Diana Palmer

"A visit to Silhouette is a guaranteed happy ending, a chance to touch magic for a little while.... It refreshes and revitalizes and makes us feel better.... I hope Silhouette goes on forever."

—Award-winning bestselling author
Marie Ferrarella

Silhouette ROMANCE™

Multi-*New York Times* bestselling author

Nora Roberts

knew from the first how to capture readers' hearts.
Celebrate the 20th Anniversary of Silhouette Books
with this special 2-in-1 edition containing her fabulous
first book and the sensational sequel.

Coming in June

Irish Hearts

Adelia Cunnane's fiery temper sets proud, powerful horse
breeder Travis Grant's heart aflame and he resolves to
make this wild *Irish Thoroughbred* his own.

Erin McKinnon accepts wealthy Burke Logan's loveless
proposal, but can this ravishing *Irish Rose* win her
hard-hearted husband's love?

Also available in June from
Silhouette Special Edition (SSE #1328)

Irish Rebel

In this brand-new sequel to *Irish Thoroughbred*, Travis and
Adelia's innocent but strong-willed daughter Keeley discovers
love in the arms of a charming Irish rogue with a talent for
horses...and romance.

Where love comes alive™